Entire contents © 2016 Anouk Ricard. Translation © 2016 Helge Dascher. Translation editor: John Kadlecek. All rights reserved. No part of this book (except small portions for review purposes) may be reproduced in any form without written permission from Anouk Ricard or Enfant. Enfant is an imprint of Drawn & Quarterly. Originally published in French as *Anna et Froga: En vadrouille* by Éditions Sarbacane. First hardcover edition: June 2016. 10 9 8 7 6 5 4 3 2 1. Printed in Malaysia. Library and Archives Canada Cataloguing in Publication: Ricard, Anouk [*Vadrouille.* English] *Out and About* / Anouk Ricard. (*Anna & Froga; 5*) Translation of: *En vadrouille.* ISBN 978-1-77046-240-3 (bound) 1. Graphic novels. I. Title. II. Title: Vadrouille. English II. Series: Ricard, Anouk. *Anna & Froga*; 5. PZ7.7.R53 Out 2016 j741.5'944 C2015-906030-3. This work, published as part of grant programs for publication (Acquisition of Rights and Translation), received support from the French Ministry of Foreign and European Affairs and from the Institut français. Cet ouvrage, publié dans le cadre du Programme d'Aide à la Publication (Cession de droits et Traduction), a bénéficié du soutien du Ministère des Affaires étrangères et européennes et de l'Institut français. Drawn & Quarterly reconnaît l'appui du gouvernement du Canada/Drawn & Quarterly acknowledges the support of the Government of Canada and the Canada Council for the Arts for our publishing program, and the National Translation Program for Book Publishing, an initiative of the Roadmap for Canada's Official Languages 2013–2018: Education, Immigration, Communities, for

Liberté • Égalité • Fraternité
RÉPUBLIQUE FRANÇAISE

our translation activities. Drawn & Quarterly reconnaît l'aide financière du gouvernement du Québec par l'entremise de la Société de développement des entreprises culturelles (SODEC) pour nos activités d'édition. Gouvernement du Québec—Programme de crédit d'impôt pour l'édition de livres—Gestion SODEC. Published in the USA by Drawn & Quarterly, a client publisher of Farrar, Straus and Giroux. Orders: 888.330.8477. Published in Canada by Drawn & Quarterly, a client publisher of Raincoast Books. Orders: 800.663.5714. Published in the United Kingdom by Drawn & Quarterly, a client publisher of Publishers Group UK. Orders: info@pguk.co.uk.

nouk Ricard

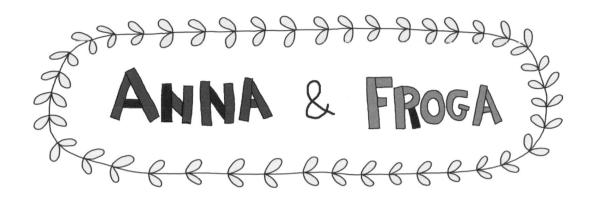

Out and about

ENFANT

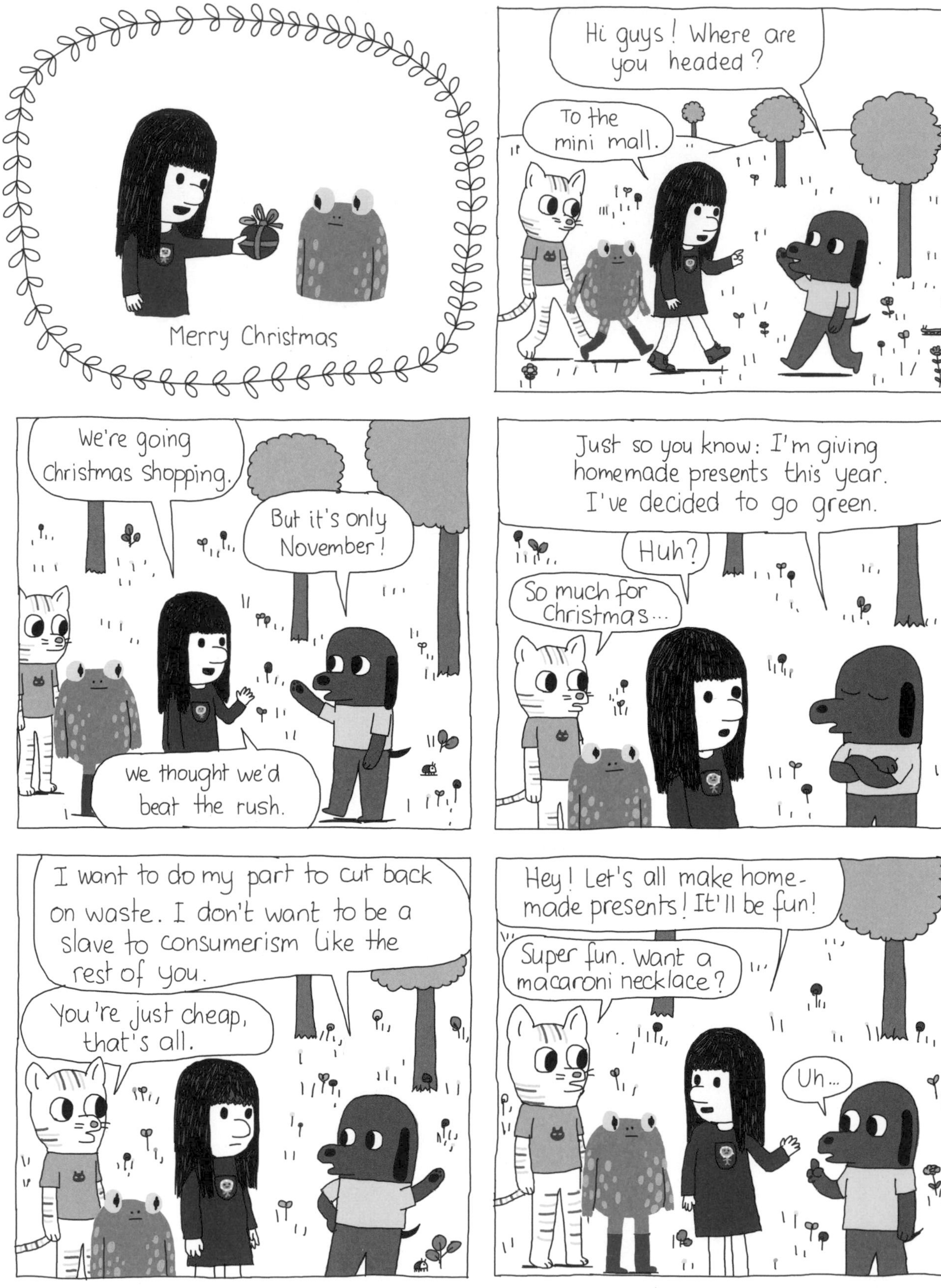
Merry Christmas
Hi guys! Where are you headed?
To the mini mall.
We're going Christmas shopping.
But it's only November!
We thought we'd beat the rush.
Just so you know: I'm giving homemade presents this year. I've decided to go green.
Huh?
So much for Christmas...
I want to do my part to cut back on waste. I don't want to be a slave to consumerism like the rest of you.
You're just cheap, that's all.
Hey! Let's all make home-made presents! It'll be fun!
Super fun. Want a macaroni necklace?
Uh...

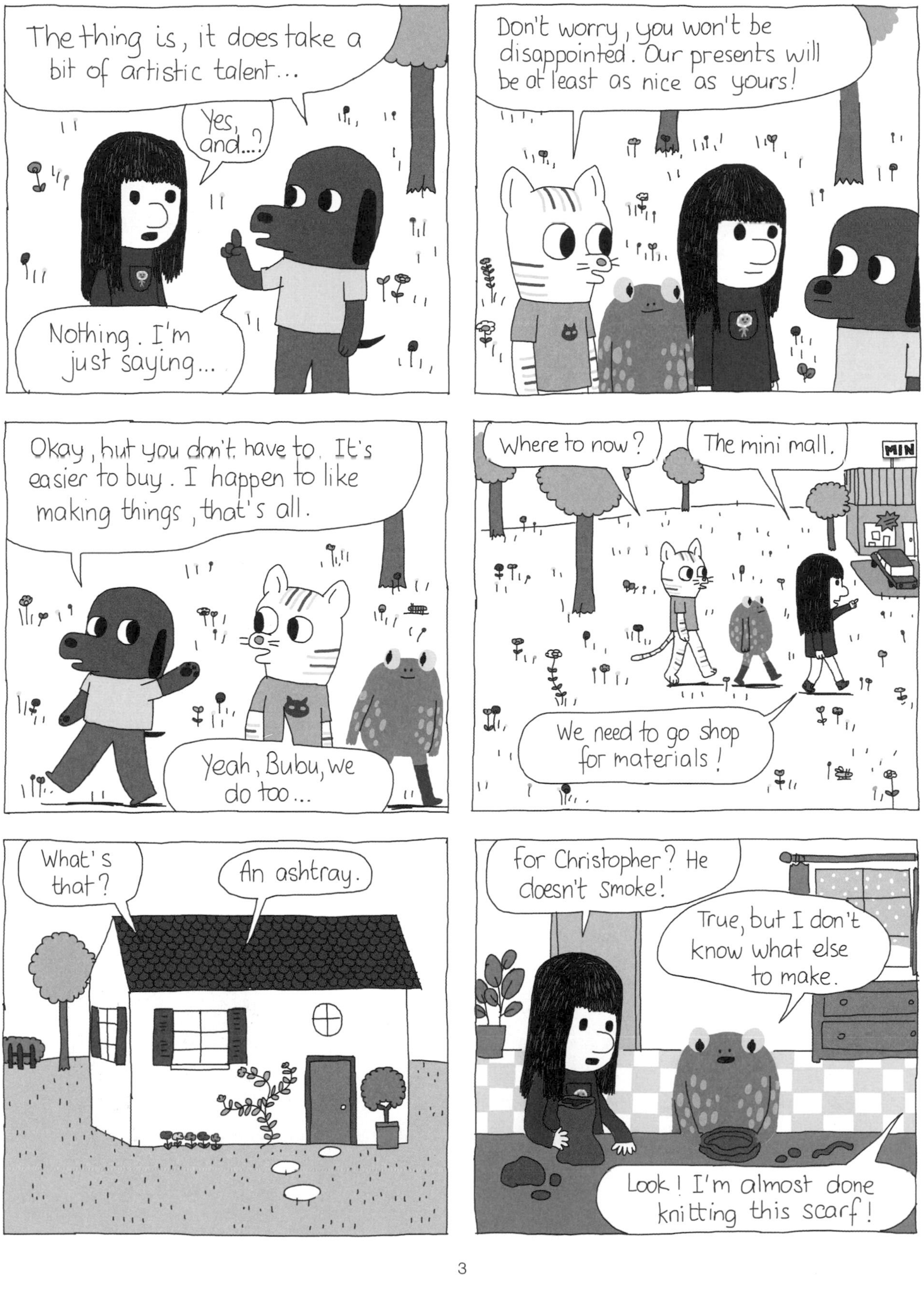
The thing is, it does take a bit of artistic talent...
Yes, and...?
Nothing. I'm just saying...
Don't worry, you won't be disappointed. Our presents will be at least as nice as yours!
Okay, but you don't have to. It's easier to buy. I happen to like making things, that's all.
Yeah, Bubu, we do too...
Where to now?
The mini mall.
We need to go shop for materials!
What's that?
An ashtray.
For Christopher? He doesn't smoke!
True, but I don't know what else to make.
Look! I'm almost done knitting this scarf!

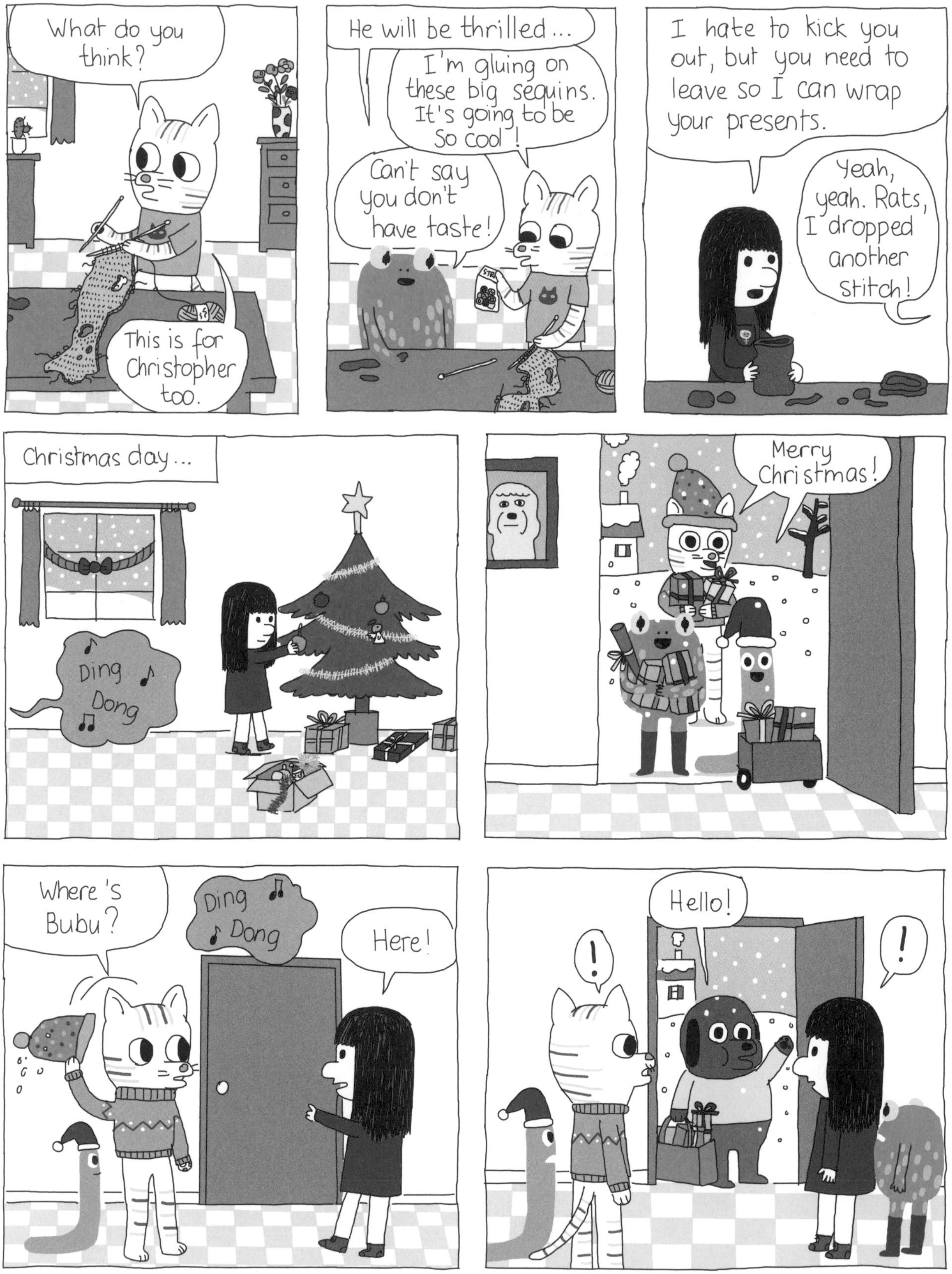
What do you think?
This is for Christopher too.
He will be thrilled...
I'm gluing on these big sequins. It's going to be so cool!
Can't say you don't have taste!
I hate to kick you out, but you need to leave so I can wrap your presents.
Yeah, yeah. Rats, I dropped another stitch!
Christmas day...
Ding Dong
Merry Christmas!
Where's Bubu?
Ding Dong
Here!
Hello!
!
!

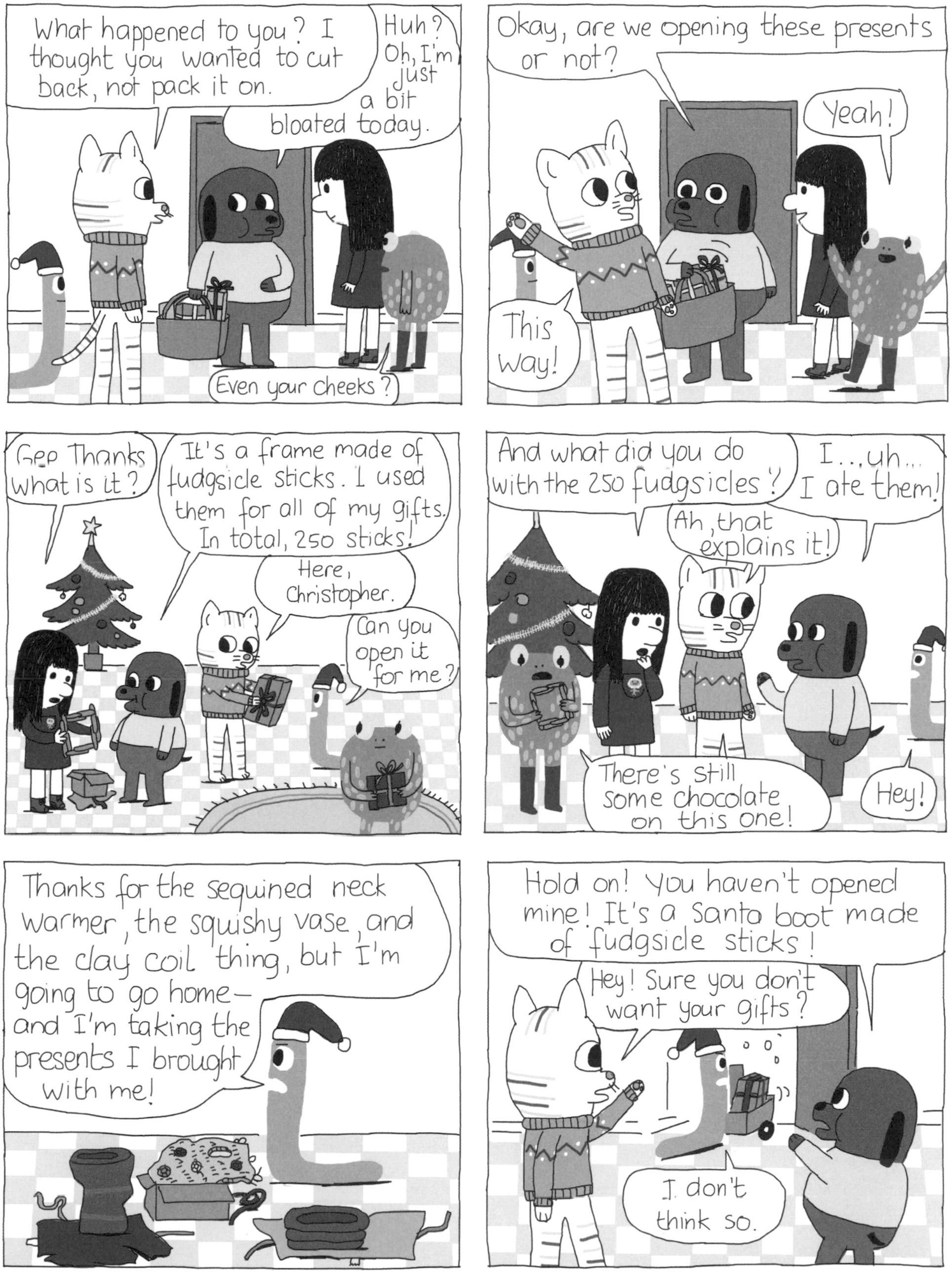
What happened to you? I thought you wanted to cut back, not pack it on.
Huh? Oh, I'm just a bit bloated today.
Even your cheeks?
Okay, are we opening these presents or not?
Yeah!
This way!
Gee Thanks what is it?
It's a frame made of fudgsicle sticks. I used them for all of my gifts. In total, 250 sticks!
Here, Christopher.
Can you open it for me?
And what did you do with the 250 fudgsicles?
I...uh... I ate them!
Ah, that explains it!
There's still some chocolate on this one!
Hey!
Thanks for the sequined neck warmer, the squishy vase, and the clay coil thing, but I'm going to go home— and I'm taking the presents I brought with me!
Hold on! You haven't opened mine! It's a Santa boot made of fudgsicle sticks!
Hey! Sure you don't want your gifts?
I don't think so.

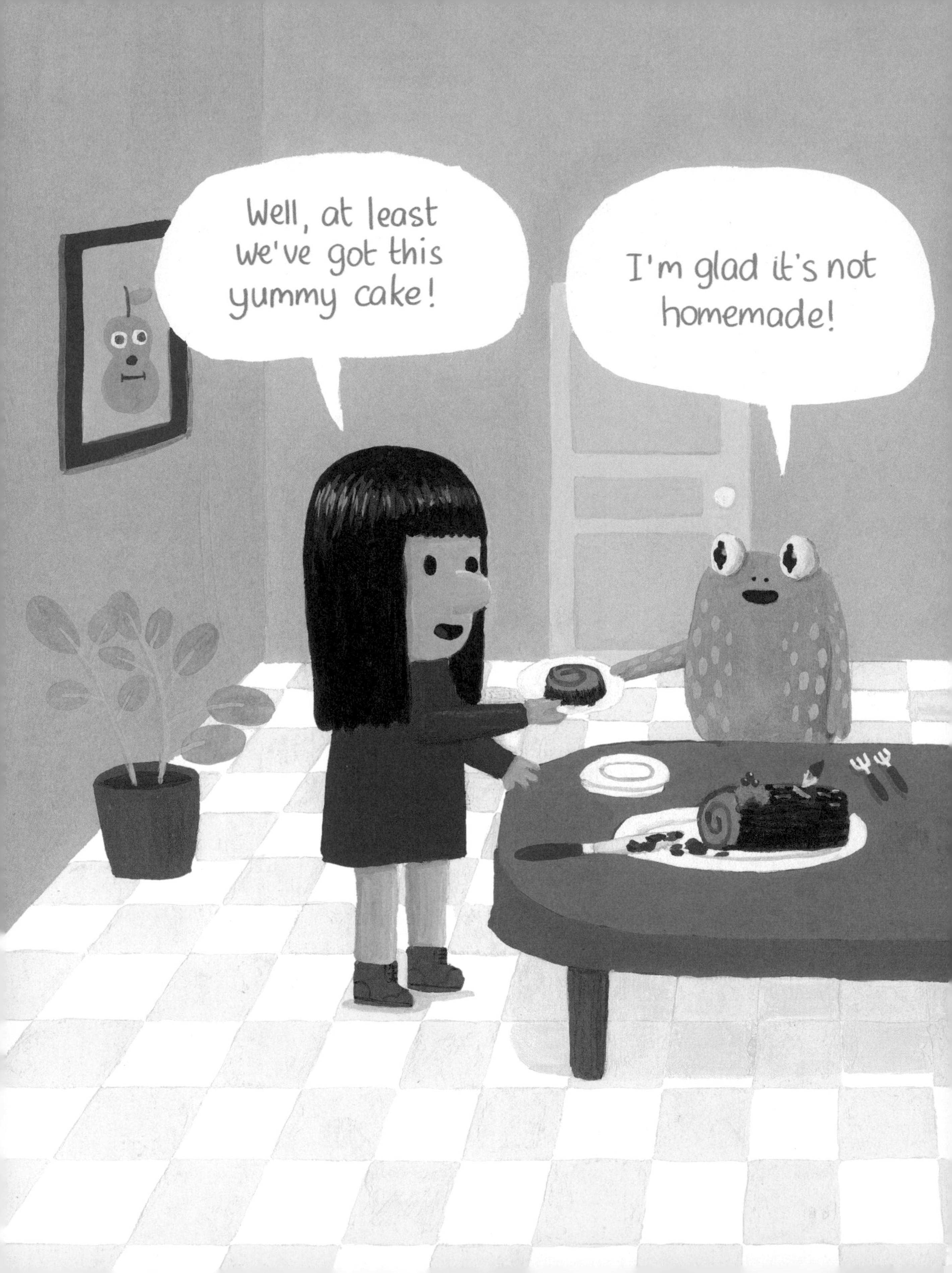
Well, at least we've got this yummy cake!
I'm glad it's not homemade!

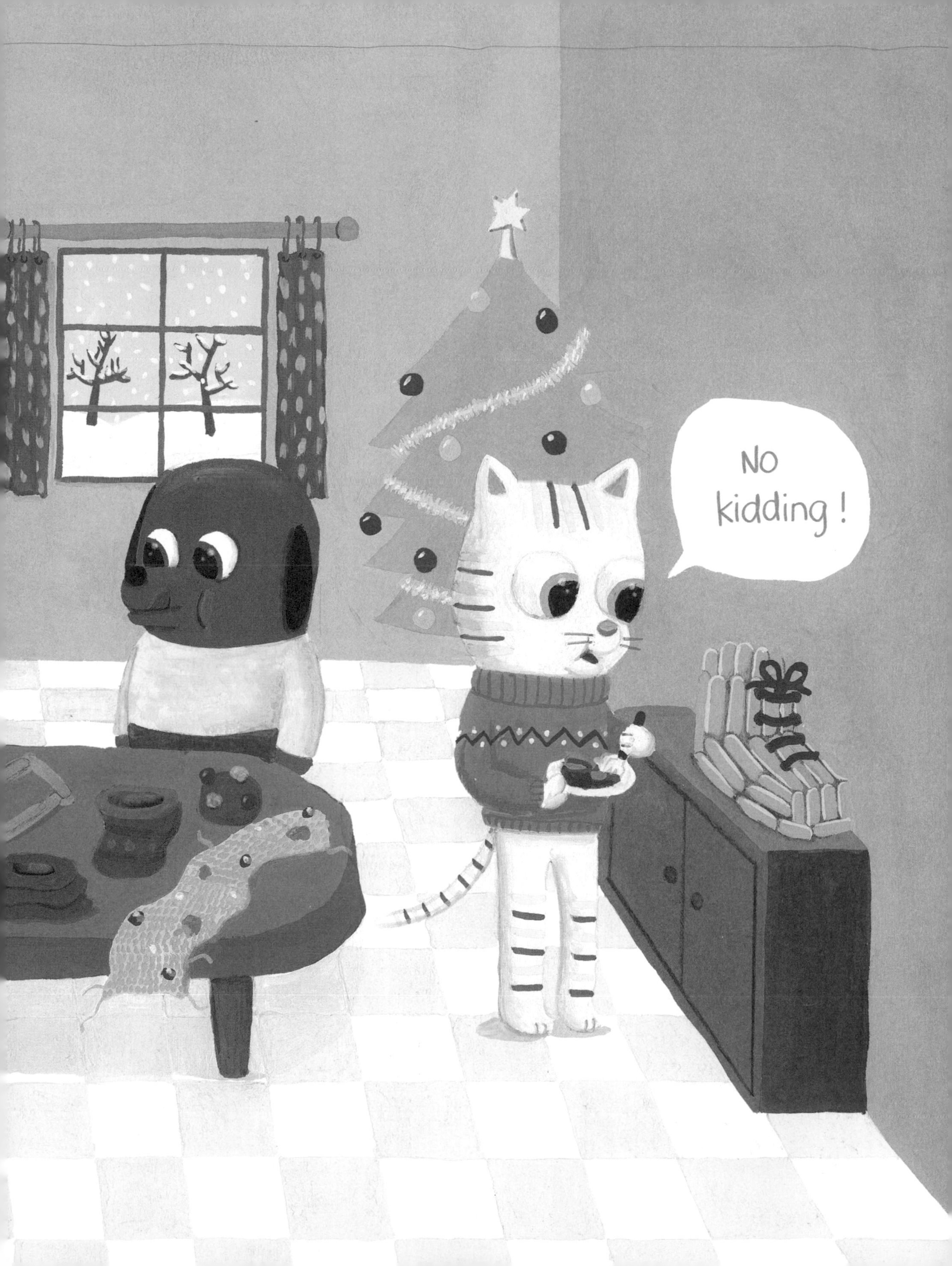
No kidding !

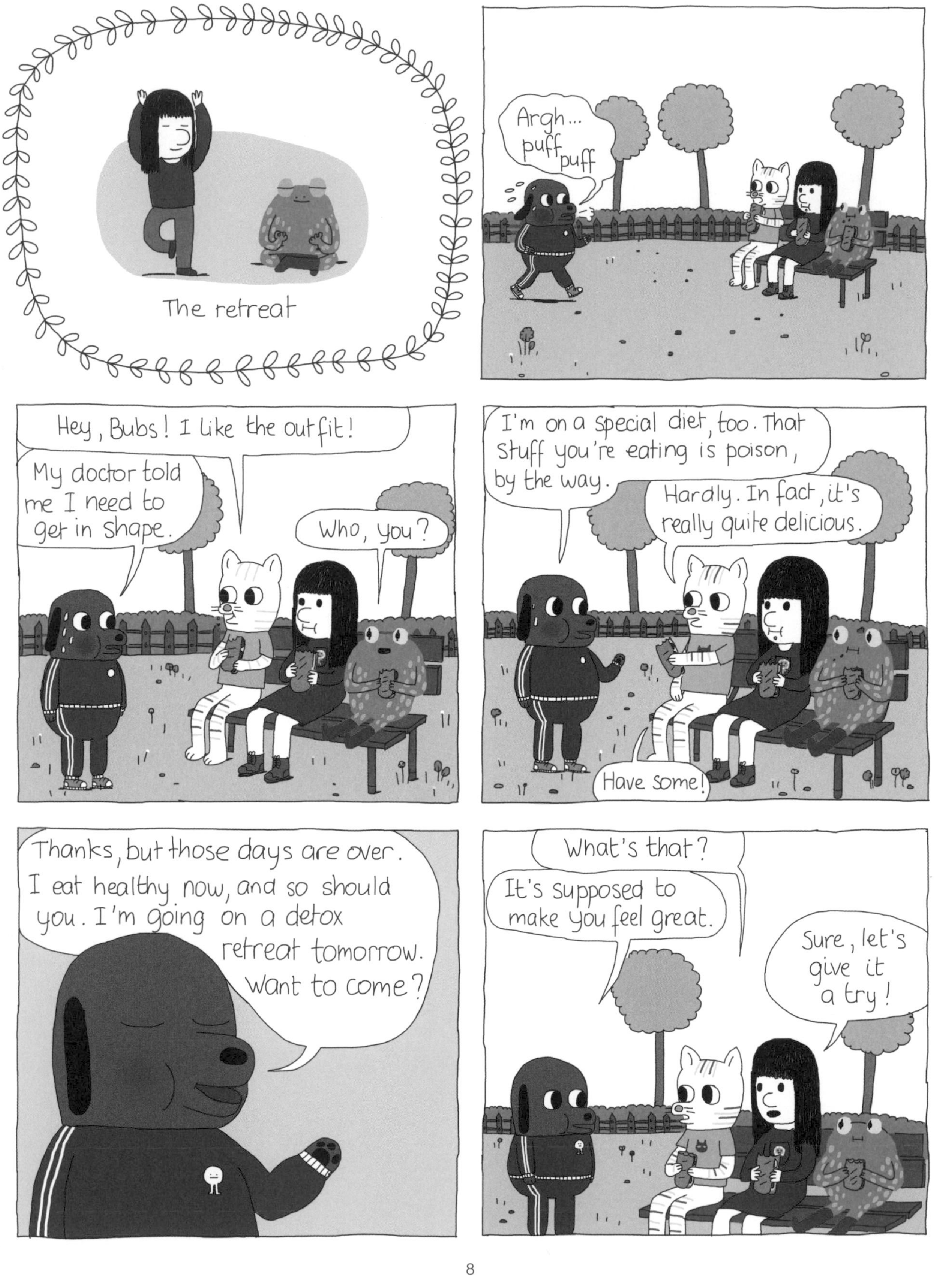
The retreat
Argh... puff puff
Hey, Bubs! I like the outfit!
My doctor told me I need to get in shape.
Who, you?
I'm on a special diet, too. That stuff you're eating is poison, by the way.
Hardly. In fact, it's really quite delicious.
Have some!
Thanks, but those days are over. I eat healthy now, and so should you. I'm going on a detox retreat tomorrow. Want to come?
What's that?
It's supposed to make you feel great.
Sure, let's give it a try!

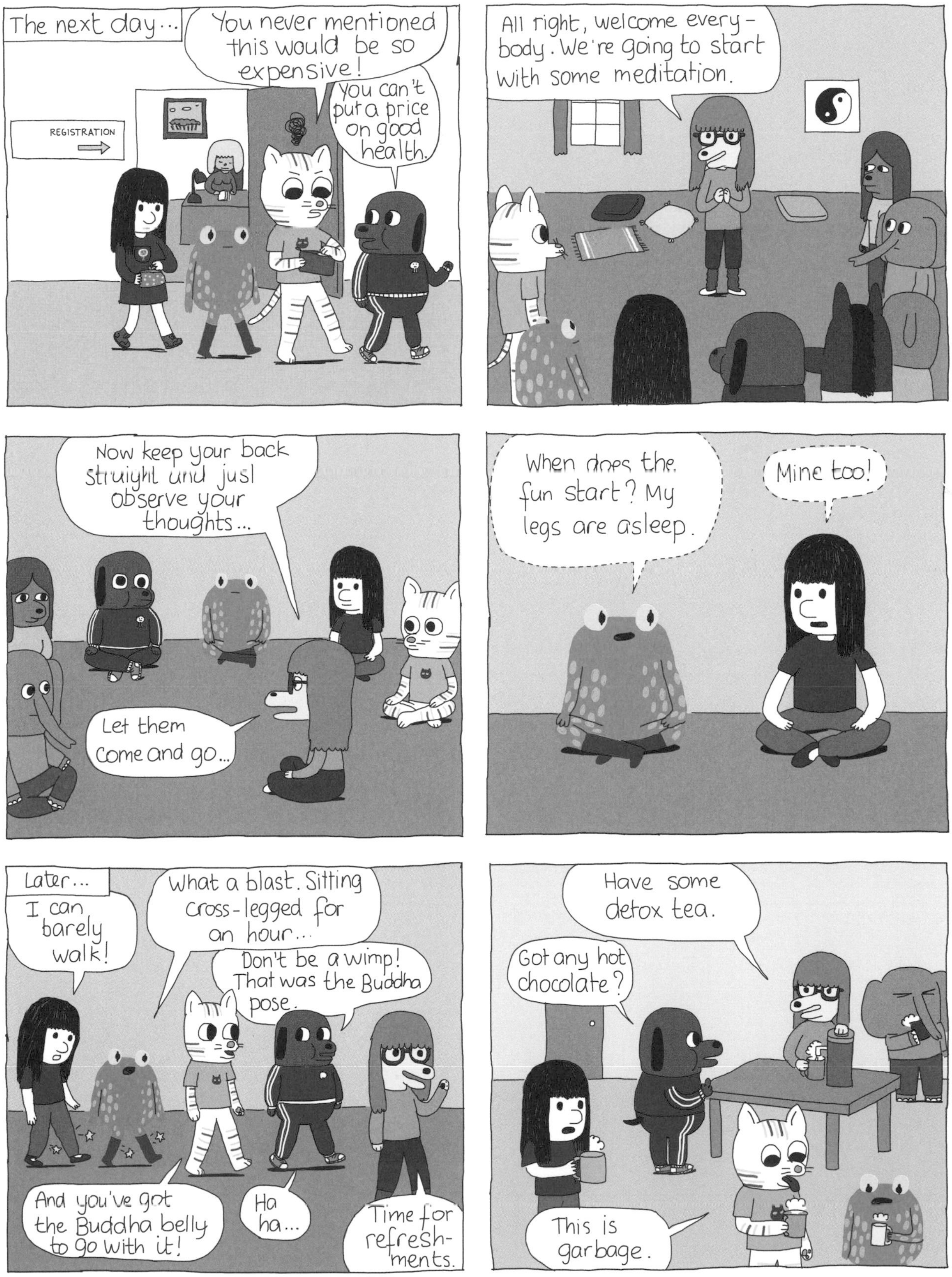
The next day...
You never mentioned this would be so expensive!
You can't put a price on good health.
REGISTRATION
All right, welcome every-body. We're going to start with some meditation.
Now keep your back straight and just observe your thoughts...
Let them come and go...
When does the fun start? My legs are asleep.
Mine too!
Later...
I can barely walk!
What a blast. Sitting cross-legged for an hour...
Don't be a wimp! That was the Buddha pose.
And you've got the Buddha belly to go with it!
Ha ha...
Time for refresh-ments.
Have some detox tea.
Got any hot chocolate?
This is garbage.

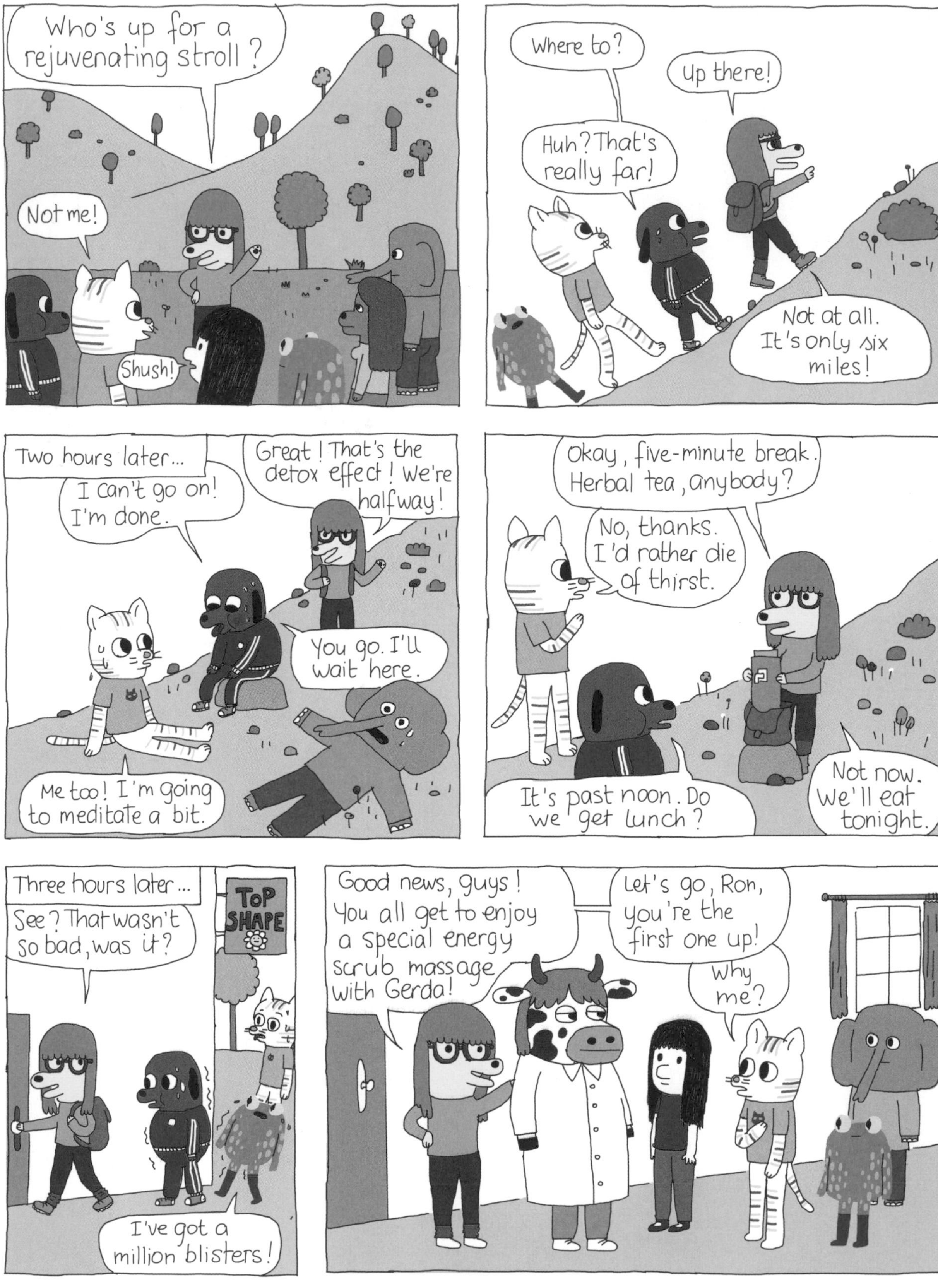
Who's up for a rejuvenating stroll?
Not me!
Shush!
Where to?
Up there!
Huh? That's really far!
Not at all. It's only six miles!
Two hours later...
I can't go on! I'm done.
Great! That's the detox effect! We're halfway!
You go. I'll wait here.
Me too! I'm going to meditate a bit.
Okay, five-minute break. Herbal tea, anybody?
No, thanks. I'd rather die of thirst.
It's past noon. Do we get lunch?
Not now. We'll eat tonight.
Three hours later...
See? That wasn't so bad, was it?
TOP SHAPE
I've got a million blisters!
Good news, guys! You all get to enjoy a special energy scrub massage with Gerda!
Let's go, Ron, you're the first one up!
Why me?

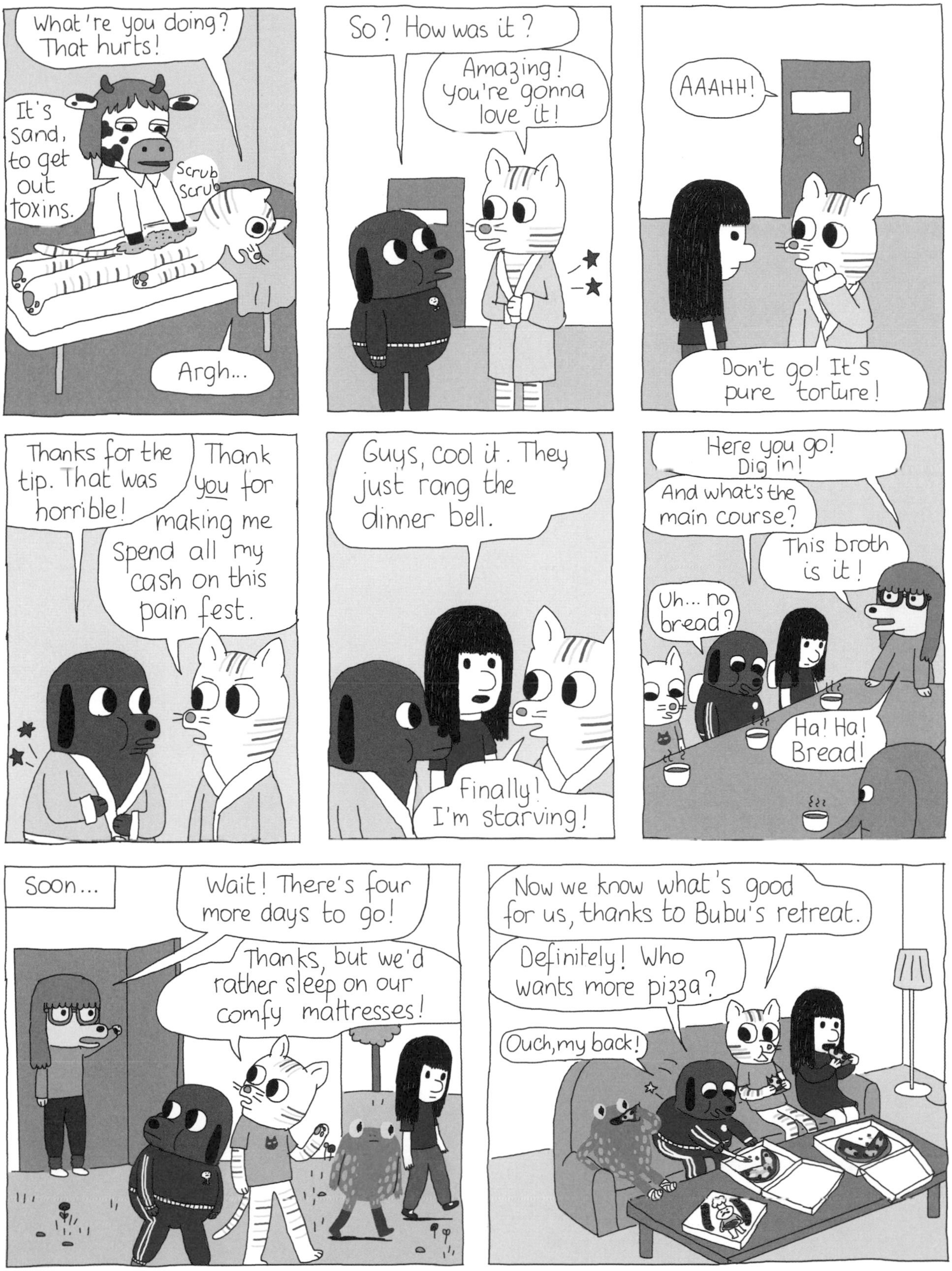
What're you doing? That hurts!
It's sand, to get out toxins.
Scrub Scrub
Argh...
So? How was it?
Amazing! You're gonna love it!
AAAHH!
Don't go! It's pure torture!
Thanks for the tip. That was horrible!
Thank you for making me spend all my cash on this pain fest.
Guys, cool it. They just rang the dinner bell.
Finally! I'm starving!
Here you go! Dig in!
And what's the main course?
This broth is it!
Uh... no bread?
Ha! Ha! Bread!
Soon...
Wait! There's four more days to go!
Thanks, but we'd rather sleep on our comfy mattresses!
Now we know what's good for us, thanks to Bubu's retreat.
Definitely! Who wants more pizza?
Ouch, my back!

Yoga with Ron and Bubu

Cobra

You're sure that's not "the otter"?

The clothespin

You're supposed to touch your toes!

My legs are too long!

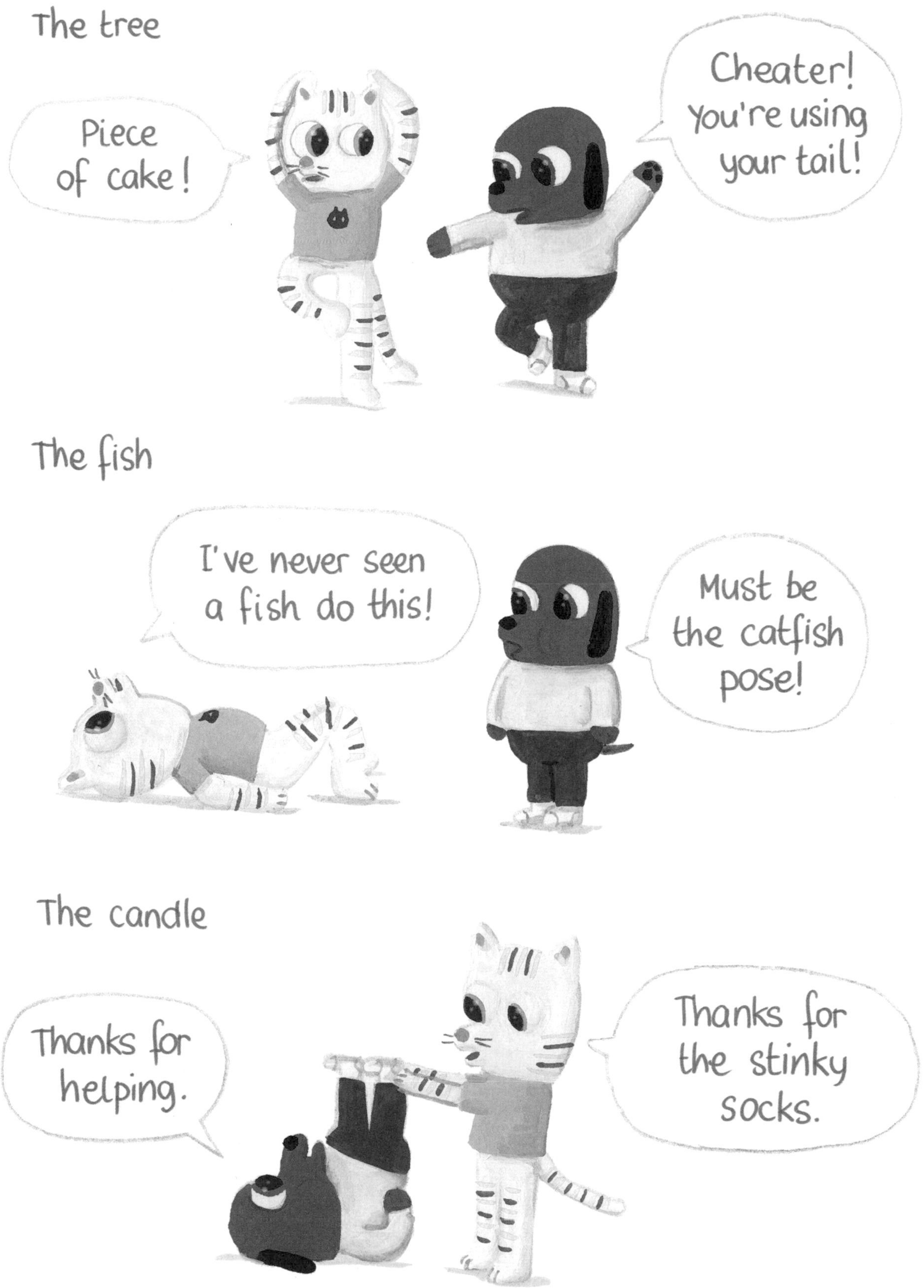
The tree
Piece of cake!
Cheater! You're using your tail!
The fish
I've never seen a fish do this!
Must be the catfish pose!
The candle
Thanks for helping.
Thanks for the stinky socks.

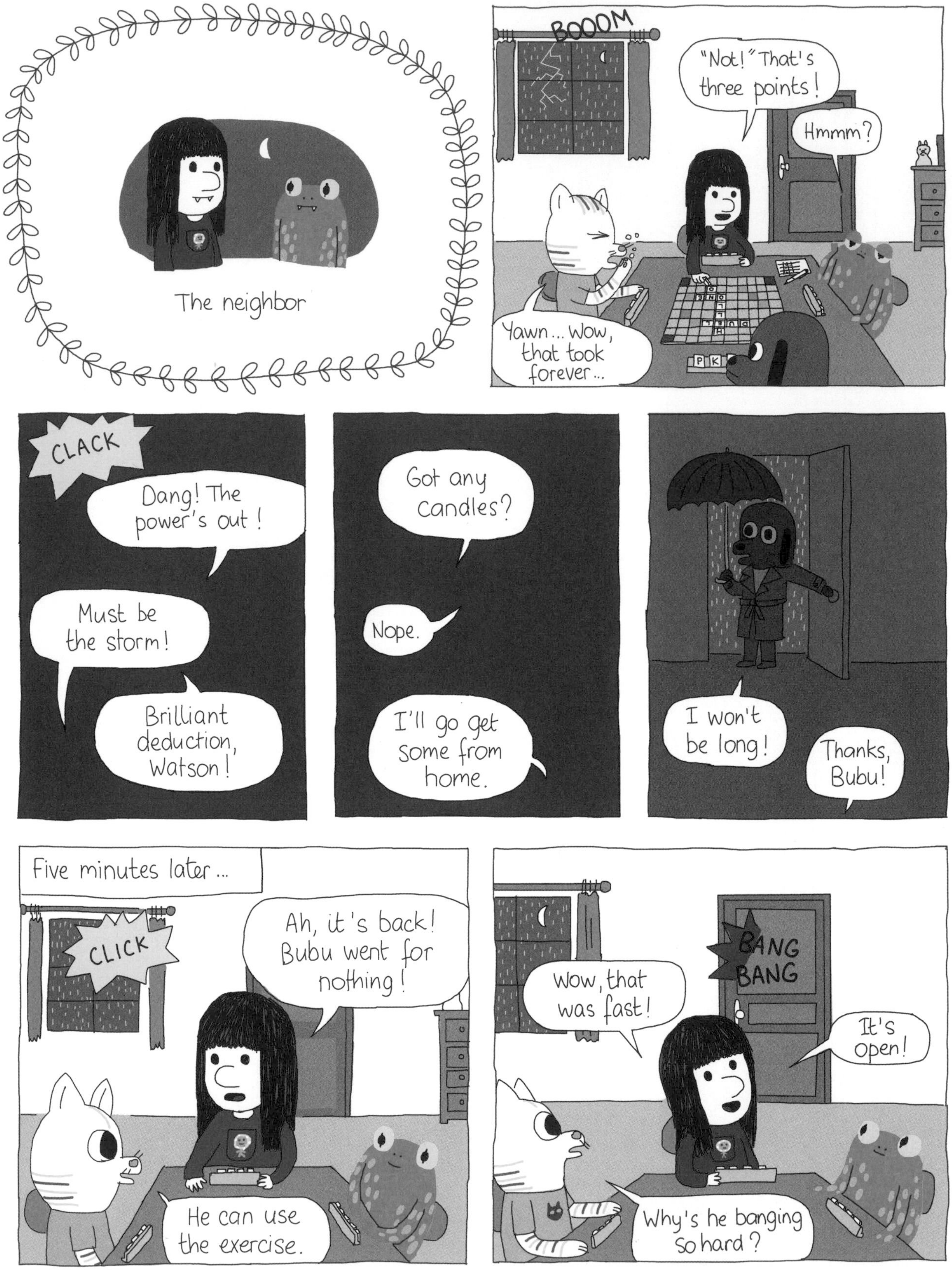
The neighbor
BOOOM
"Not!" That's three points!
Hmmm?
Yawn... Wow, that took forever...
CLACK
Dang! The power's out!
Must be the storm!
Brilliant deduction, Watson!
Got any candles?
Nope.
I'll go get some from home.
I won't be long!
Thanks, Bubu!
Five minutes later...
CLICK
Ah, it's back! Bubu went for nothing!
He can use the exercise.
BANG BANG
Wow, that was fast!
It's open!
Why's he banging so hard?

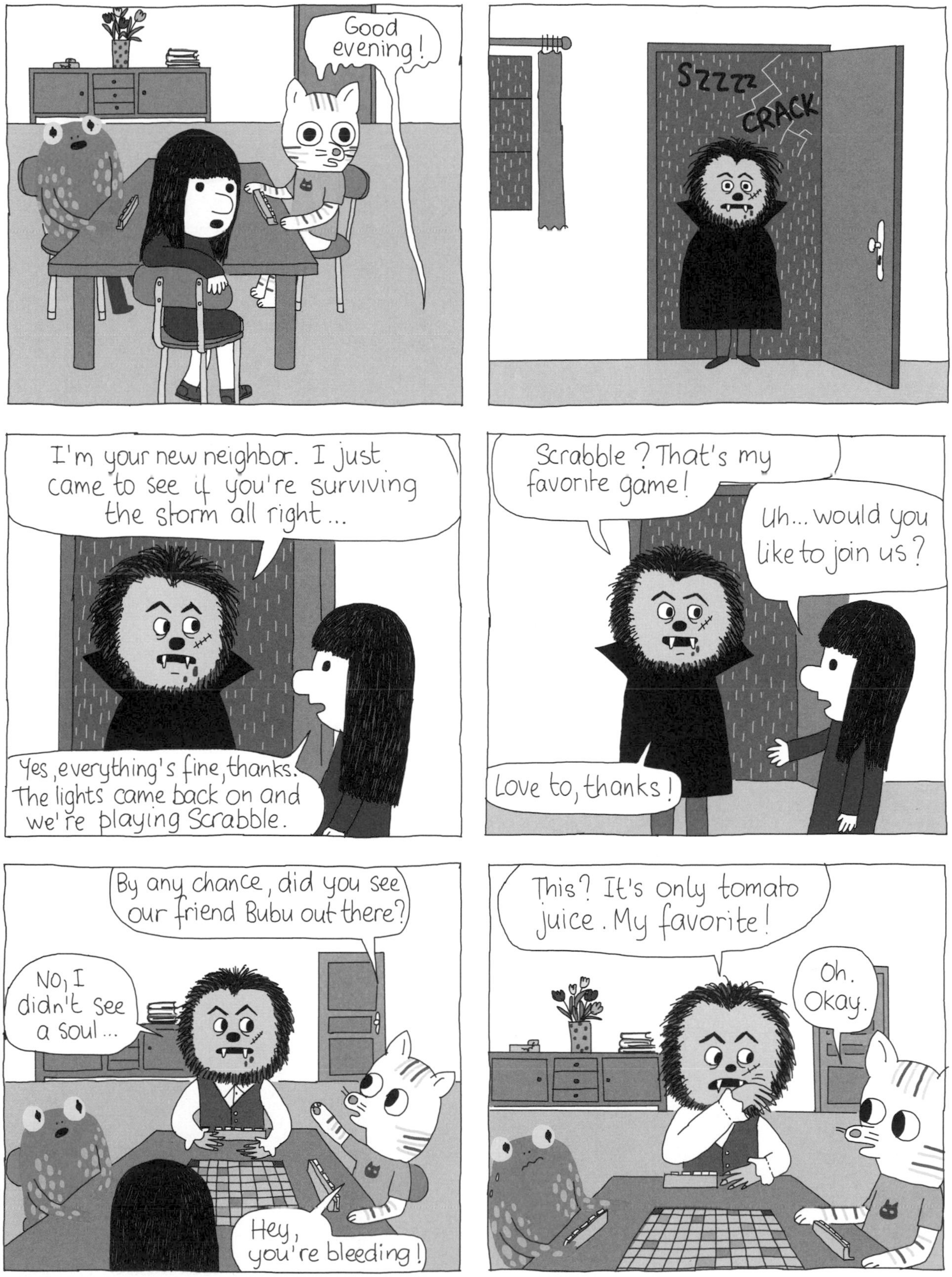
Good evening!
Szzzz
CRACK
I'm your new neighbor. I just came to see if you're surviving the storm all right...
Yes, everything's fine, thanks. The lights came back on and we're playing Scrabble.
Scrabble? That's my favorite game!
Uh... would you like to join us?
Love to, thanks!
By any chance, did you see our friend Bubu out there?
No, I didn't see a soul...
Hey, you're bleeding!
This? It's only tomato juice. My favorite!
Oh. Okay.

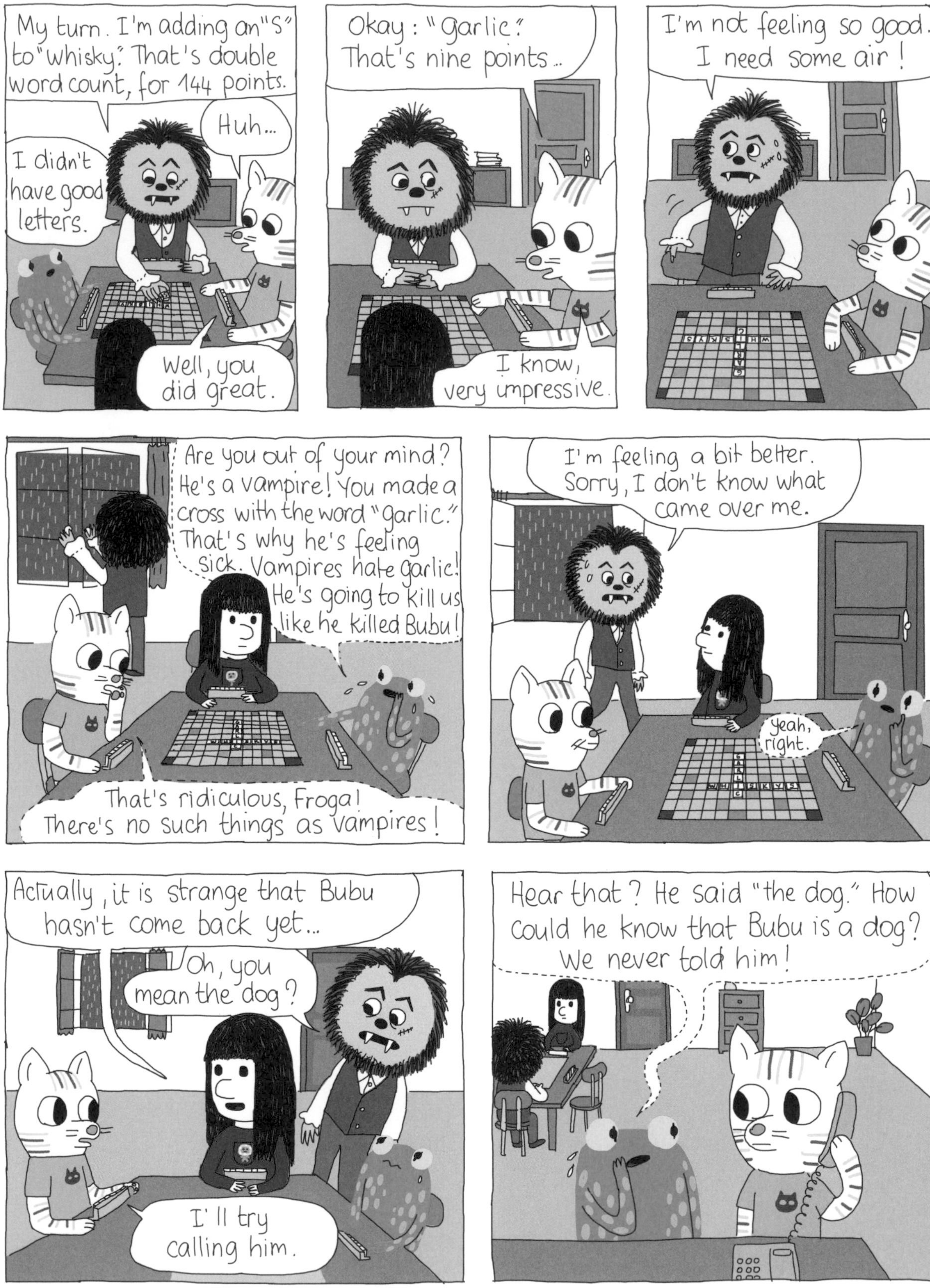
My turn. I'm adding an "S" to "whisky." That's double word count, for 144 points.
Huh...
I didn't have good letters.
Well, you did great.
Okay: "garlic." That's nine points...
I know, very impressive.
I'm not feeling so good. I need some air!
Are you out of your mind? He's a vampire! You made a cross with the word "garlic." That's why he's feeling sick. Vampires hate garlic! He's going to kill us like he killed Bubu!
That's ridiculous, Froga! There's no such things as vampires!
I'm feeling a bit better. Sorry, I don't know what came over me.
Yeah, right.
Actually, it is strange that Bubu hasn't come back yet...
Oh, you mean the dog?
I'll try calling him.
Hear that? He said "the dog." How could he know that Bubu is a dog? We never told him!

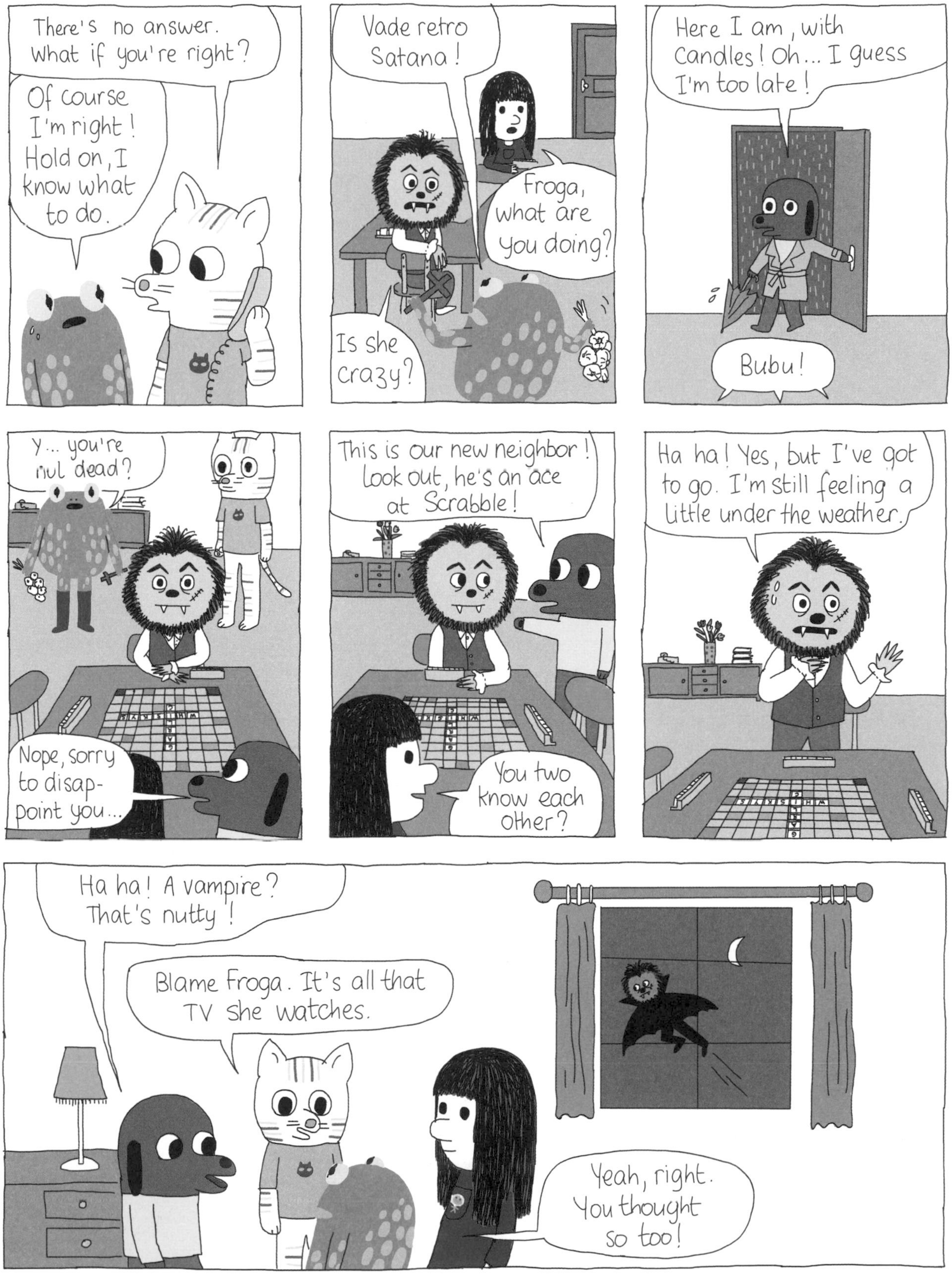
There's no answer. What if you're right?
Of course I'm right! Hold on, I know what to do.
Vade retro Satana!
Froga, what are you doing?
Is she crazy?
Here I am, with candles! Oh... I guess I'm too late!
Bubu!
Y... you're nul dead?
Nope, sorry to disap-point you...
This is our new neighbor! Look out, he's an ace at Scrabble!
You two know each other?
Ha ha! Yes, but I've got to go. I'm still feeling a little under the weather.
Ha ha! A vampire? That's nutty!
Blame Froga. It's all that TV she watches.
Yeah, right. You thought so too!

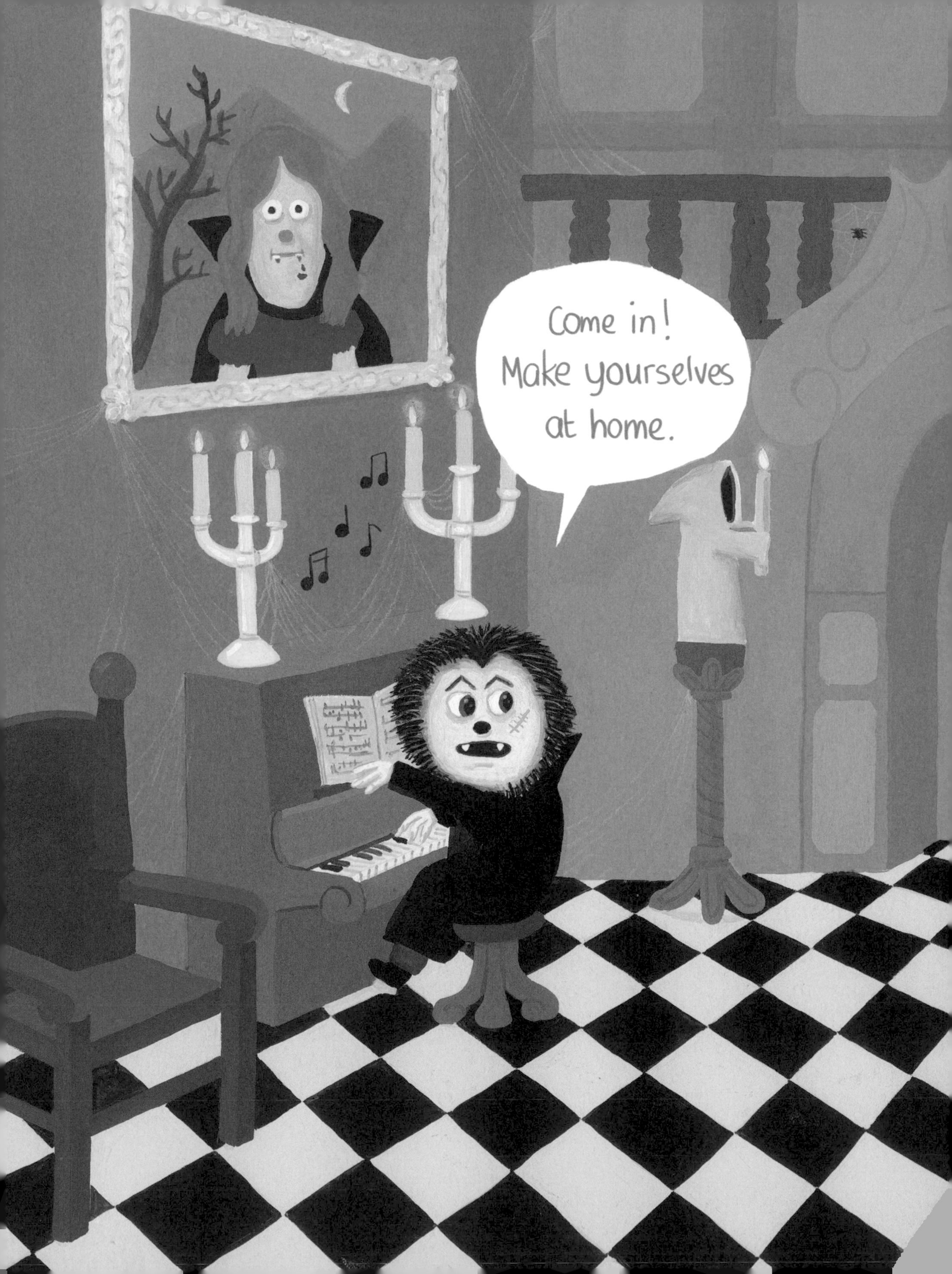
Come in! Make yourselves at home.

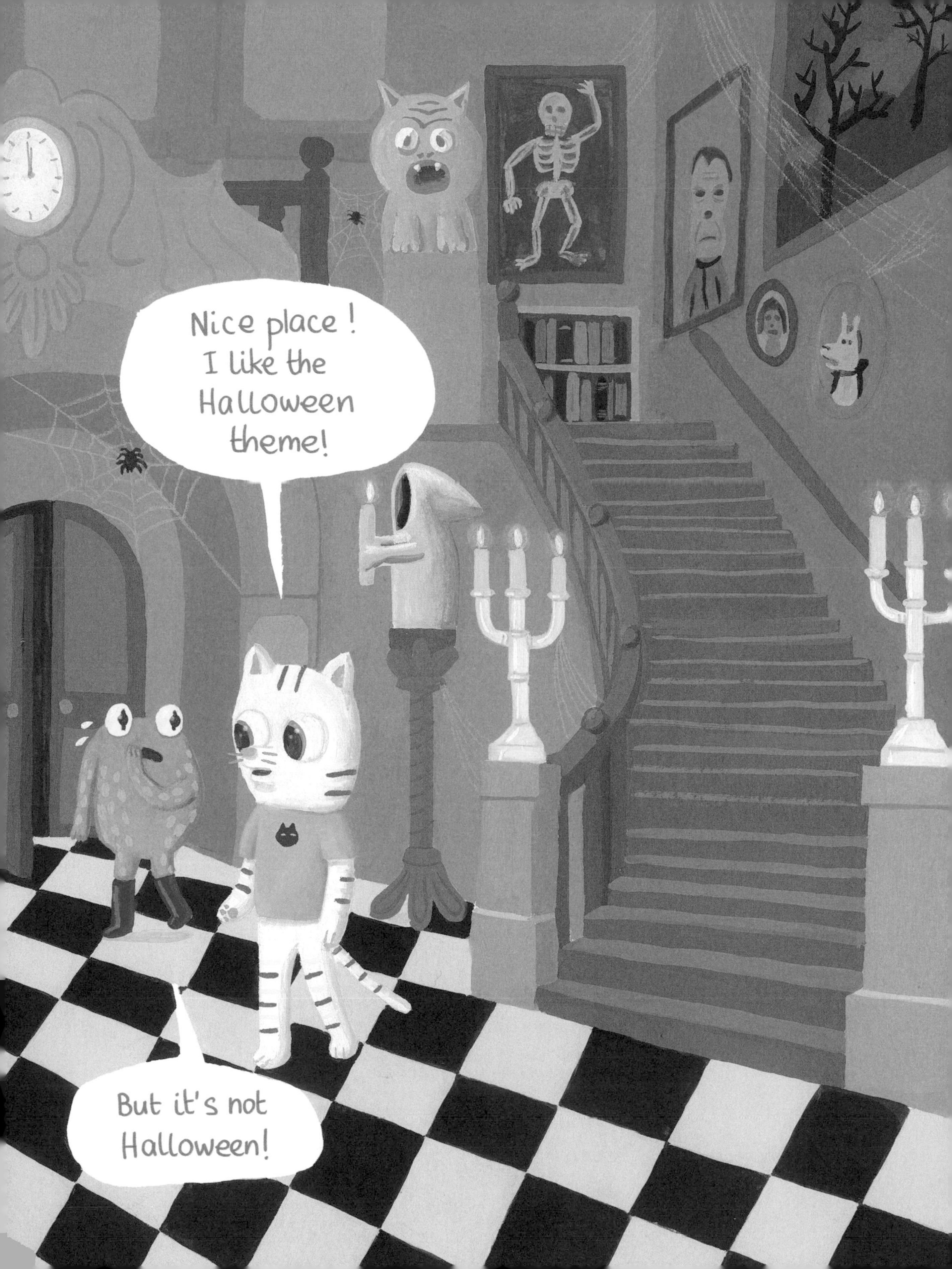
Nice place ! I like the Halloween theme!
But it's not Halloween!

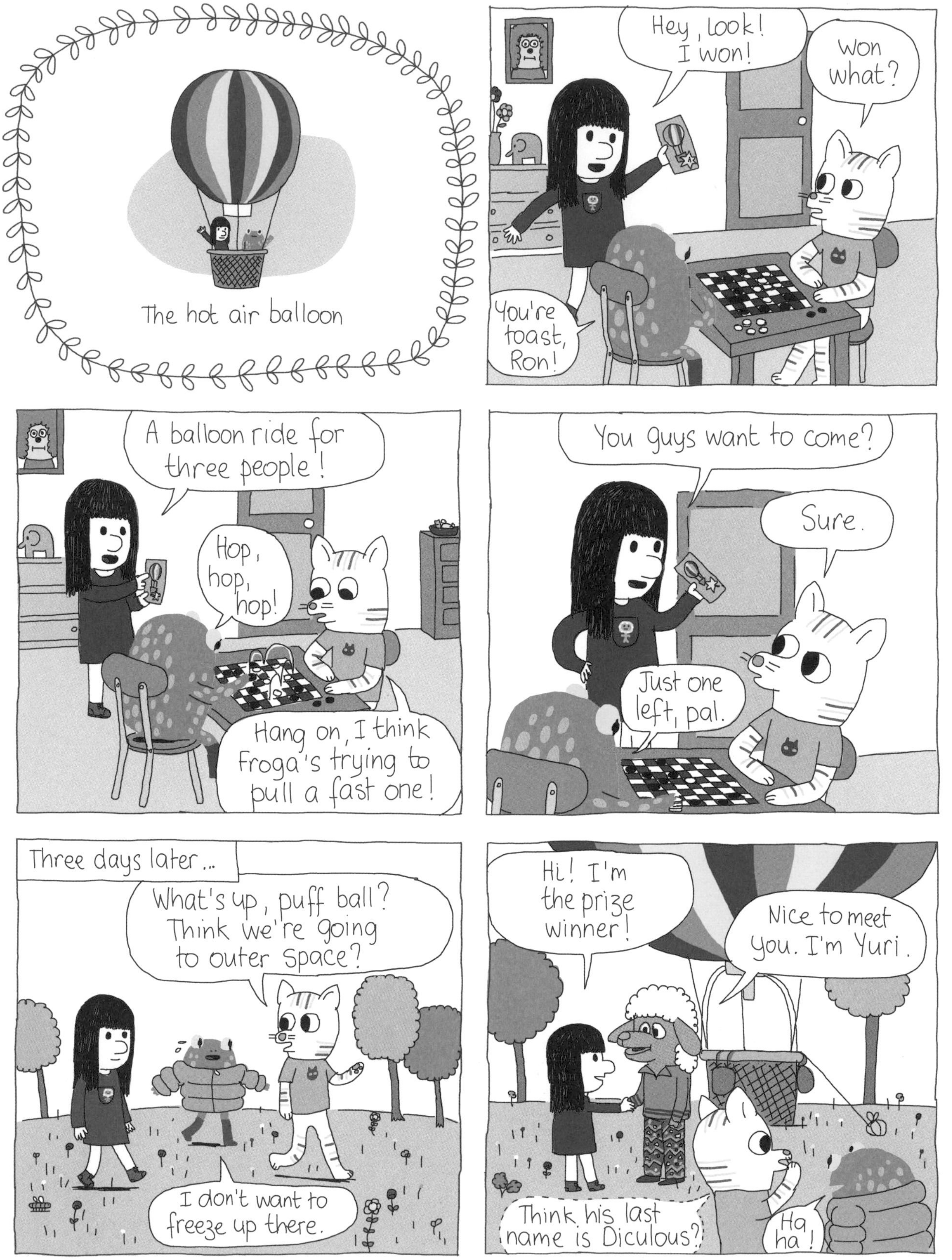
The hot air balloon
Hey, look! I won!
Won what?
You're toast, Ron!
A balloon ride for three people!
Hop, hop, hop!
Hang on, I think Froga's trying to pull a fast one!
You guys want to come?
Sure.
Just one left, pal.
Three days later...
What's up, puff ball? Think we're going to outer space?
I don't want to freeze up there.
Hi! I'm the prize winner!
Nice to meet you. I'm Yuri.
Think his last name is Diculous?
Ha ha!

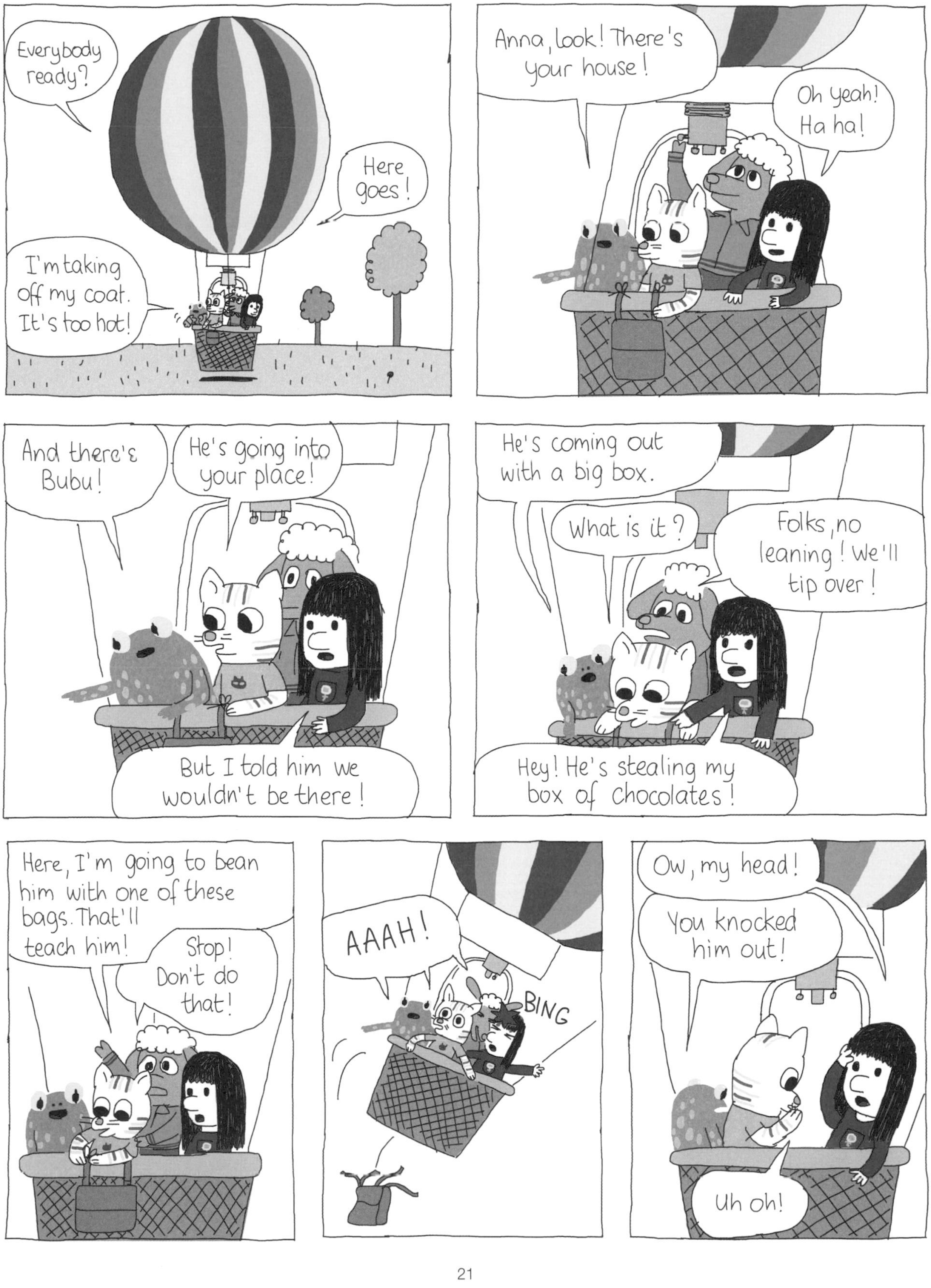

Everybody ready?
Here goes!
I'm taking off my coat. It's too hot!
Anna, look! There's your house!
Oh yeah! Ha ha!
And there's Bubu!
He's going into your place!
But I told him we wouldn't be there!
He's coming out with a big box.
What is it?
Folks, no leaning! We'll tip over!
Hey! He's stealing my box of chocolates!
Here, I'm going to bean him with one of these bags. That'll teach him!
Stop! Don't do that!
AAAH!
BING
Ow, my head!
You knocked him out!
Uh oh!

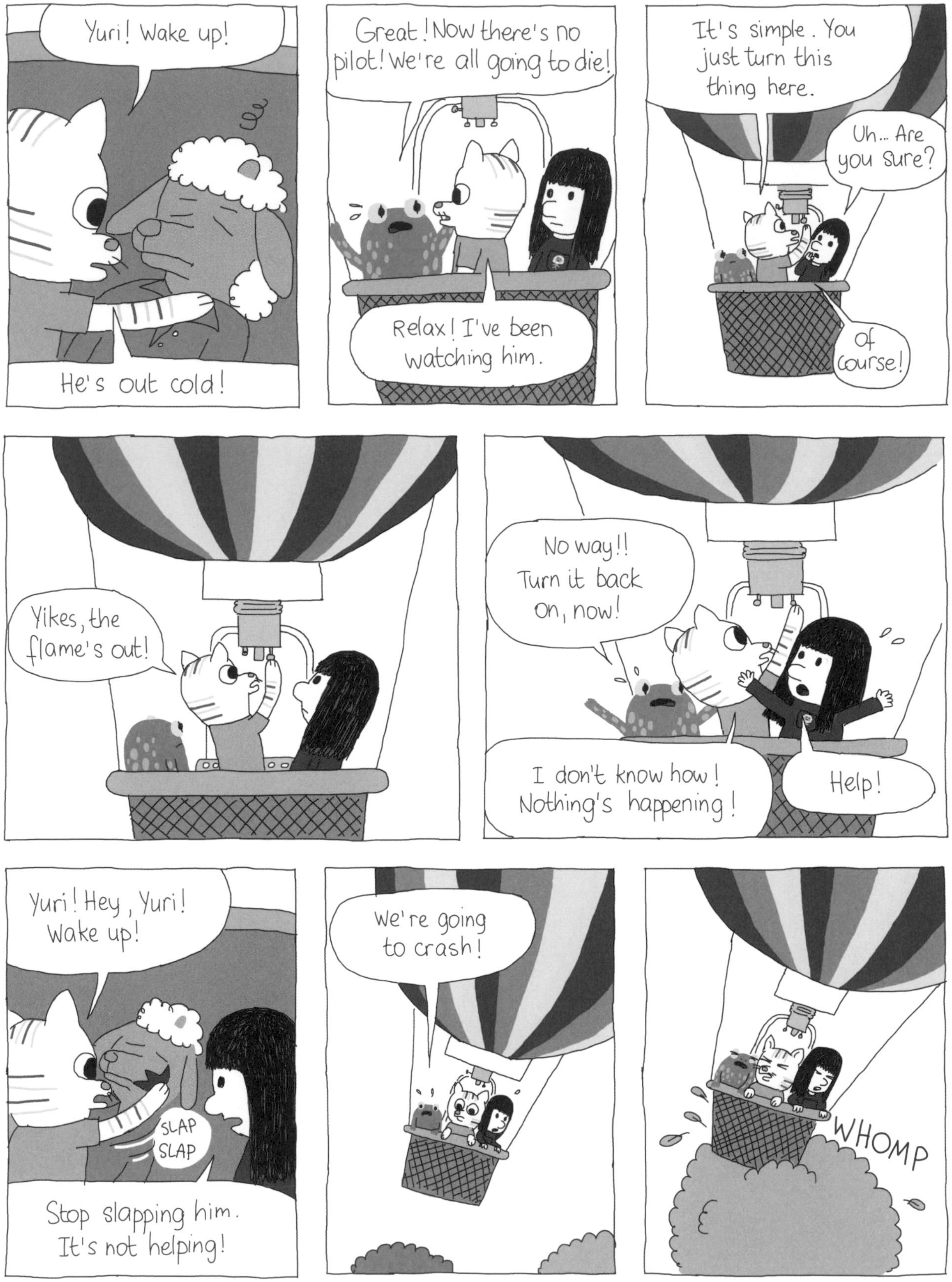

Yuri! Wake up!
He's out cold!
Great! Now there's no pilot! We're all going to die!
Relax! I've been watching him.
It's simple. You just turn this thing here.
Uh... Are you sure?
Of course!
Yikes, the flame's out!
No way!! Turn it back on, now!
I don't know how! Nothing's happening!
Help!
Yuri! Hey, Yuri! Wake up!
SLAP SLAP
Stop slapping him. It's not helping!
We're going to crash!
WHOMP

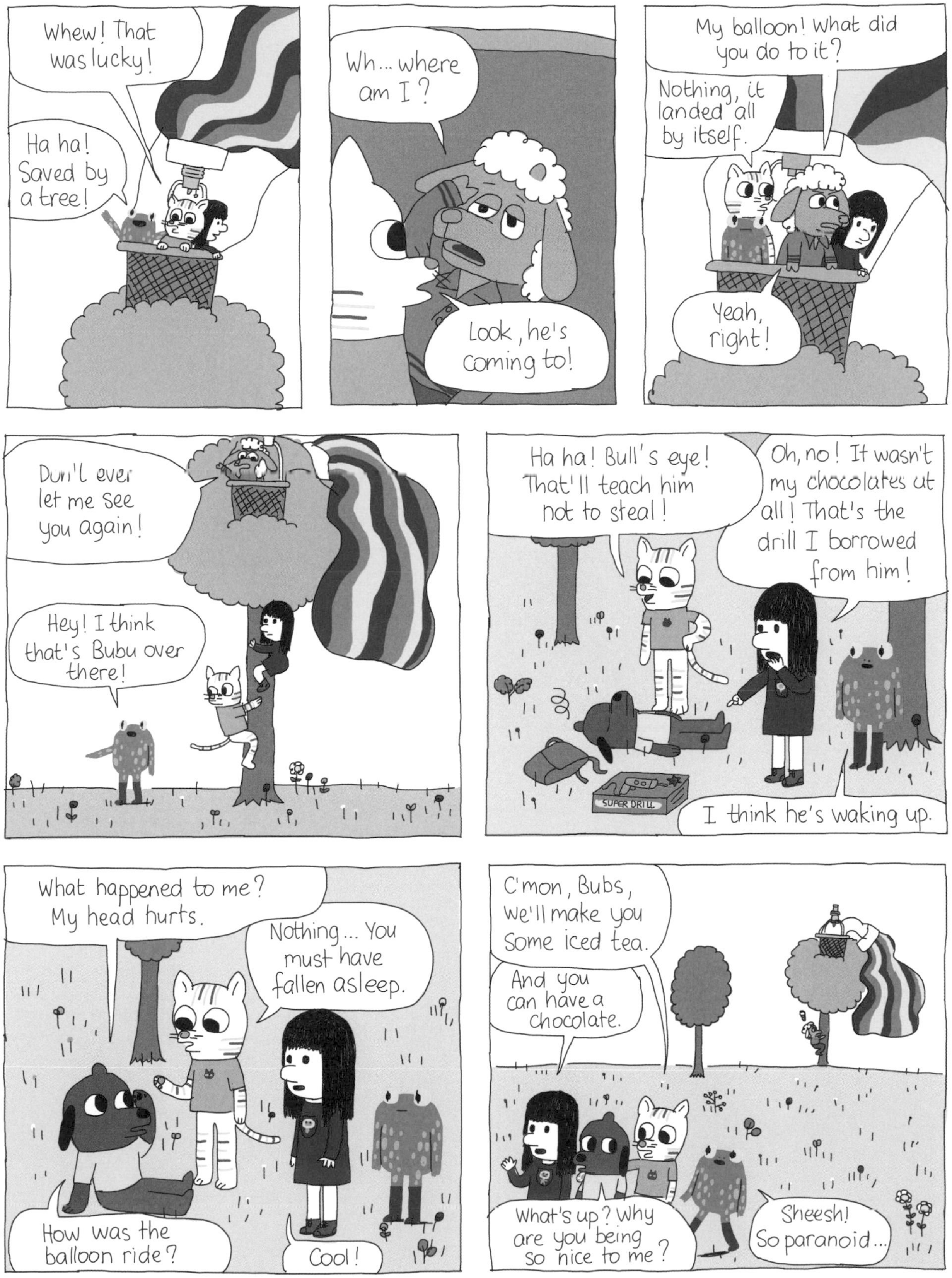
Whew! That was lucky!
Ha ha! Saved by a tree!
Wh... where am I?
Look, he's coming to!
My balloon! What did you do to it?
Nothing, it landed all by itself.
Yeah, right!
Don't ever let me see you again!
Hey! I think that's Bubu over there!
Ha ha! Bull's eye! That'll teach him not to steal!
Oh, no! It wasn't my chocolates at all! That's the drill I borrowed from him!
SUPER DRILL
I think he's waking up.
What happened to me? My head hurts.
Nothing... You must have fallen asleep.
How was the balloon ride?
Cool!
C'mon, Bubs, we'll make you some iced tea.
And you can have a chocolate.
What's up? Why are you being so nice to me?
Sheesh! So paranoid...

Balloon Safety Rules

NO

NO

NO

NO

NO

NO

NO

YES

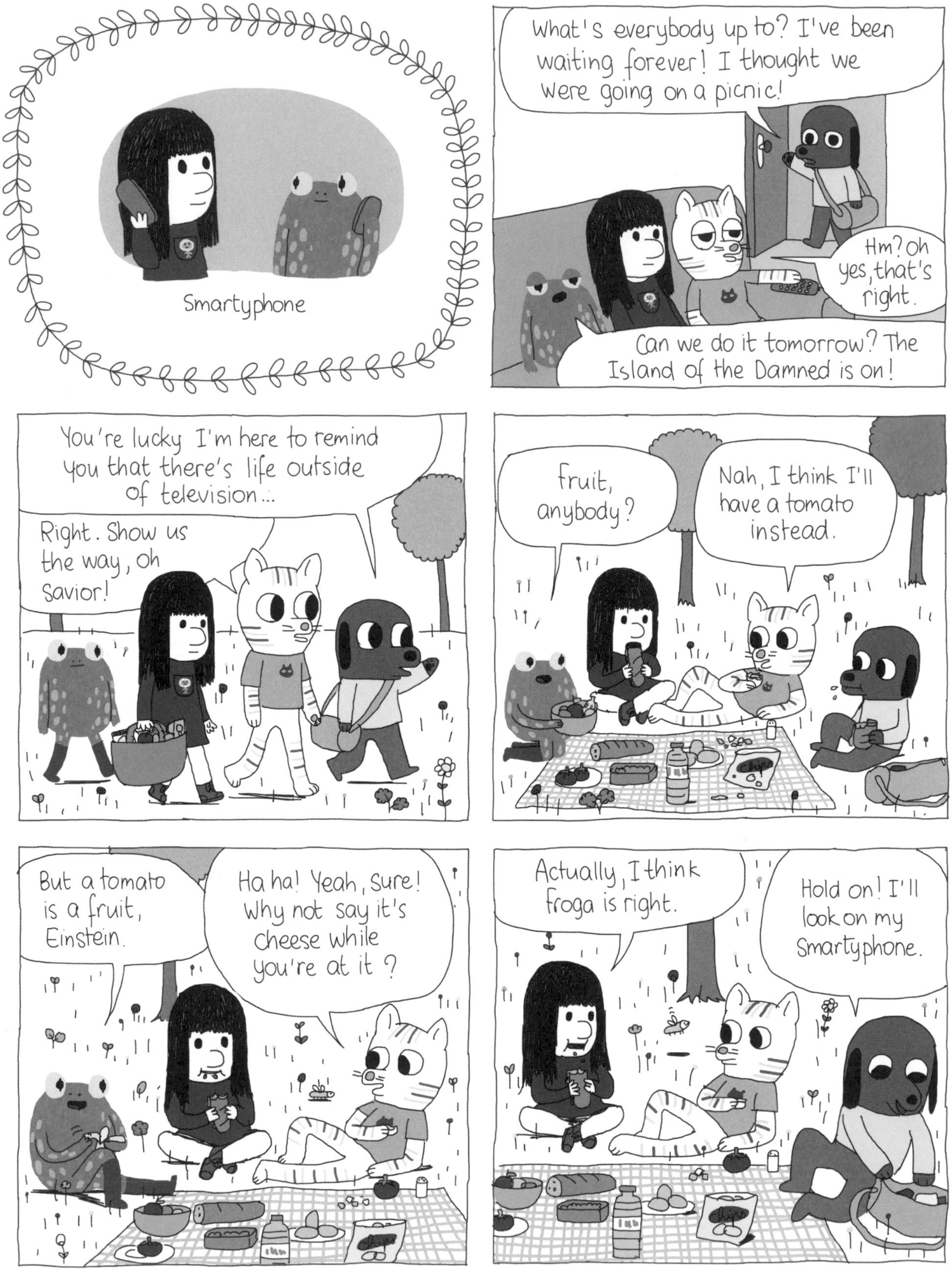
Smartyphone
What's everybody up to? I've been waiting forever! I thought we were going on a picnic!
Hm? oh yes, that's right.
Can we do it tomorrow? The Island of the Damned is on!
You're lucky I'm here to remind you that there's life outside of television...
Right. Show us the way, oh savior!
fruit, anybody?
Nah, I think I'll have a tomato instead.
But a tomato is a fruit, Einstein.
Ha ha! Yeah, sure! Why not say it's cheese while you're at it?
Actually, I think froga is right.
Hold on! I'll look on my Smartyphone.

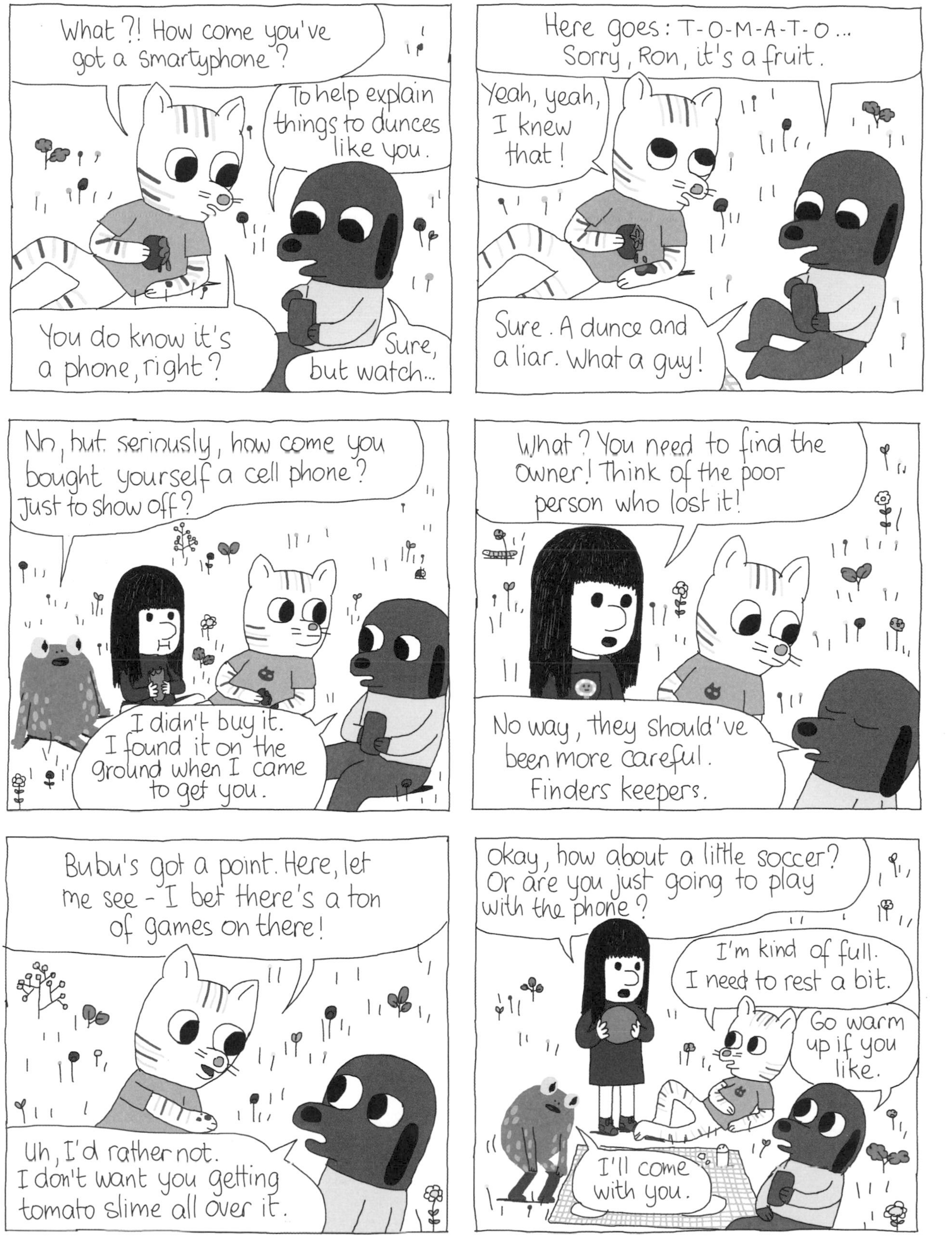
What?! How come you've got a smartyphone?
To help explain things to dunces like you.
You do know it's a phone, right?
Sure, but watch...
Here goes: T-O-M-A-T-O... Sorry, Ron, it's a fruit.
Yeah, yeah, I knew that!
Sure. A dunce and a liar. What a guy!
No, but seriously, how come you bought yourself a cell phone? Just to show off?
I didn't buy it. I found it on the ground when I came to get you.
What? You need to find the owner! Think of the poor person who lost it!
No way, they should've been more careful. Finders keepers.
Bubu's got a point. Here, let me see - I bet there's a ton of games on there!
Uh, I'd rather not. I don't want you getting tomato slime all over it.
Okay, how about a little soccer? Or are you just going to play with the phone?
I'm kind of full. I need to rest a bit.
Go warm up if you like.
I'll come with you.

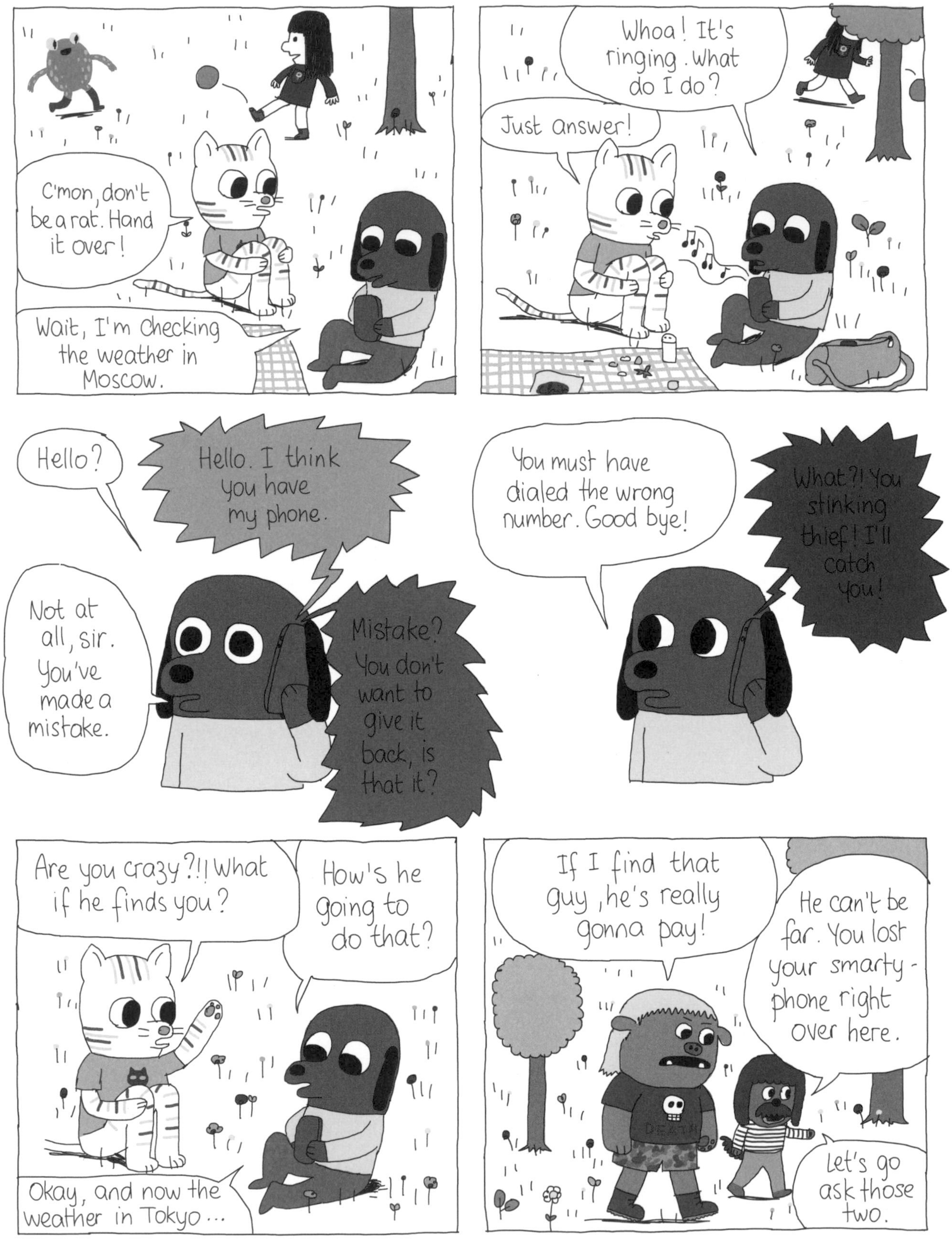
C'mon, don't be a rat. Hand it over!
Wait, I'm checking the weather in Moscow.
Whoa! It's ringing. What do I do?
Just answer!
Hello?
Hello. I think you have my phone.
Not at all, sir. You've made a mistake.
Mistake? You don't want to give it back, is that it?
You must have dialed the wrong number. Good bye!
What?! You stinking thief! I'll catch you!
Are you crazy?!! What if he finds you?
How's he going to do that?
Okay, and now the weather in Tokyo...
If I find that guy, he's really gonna pay!
He can't be far. You lost your smarty-phone right over here.
Let's go ask those two.

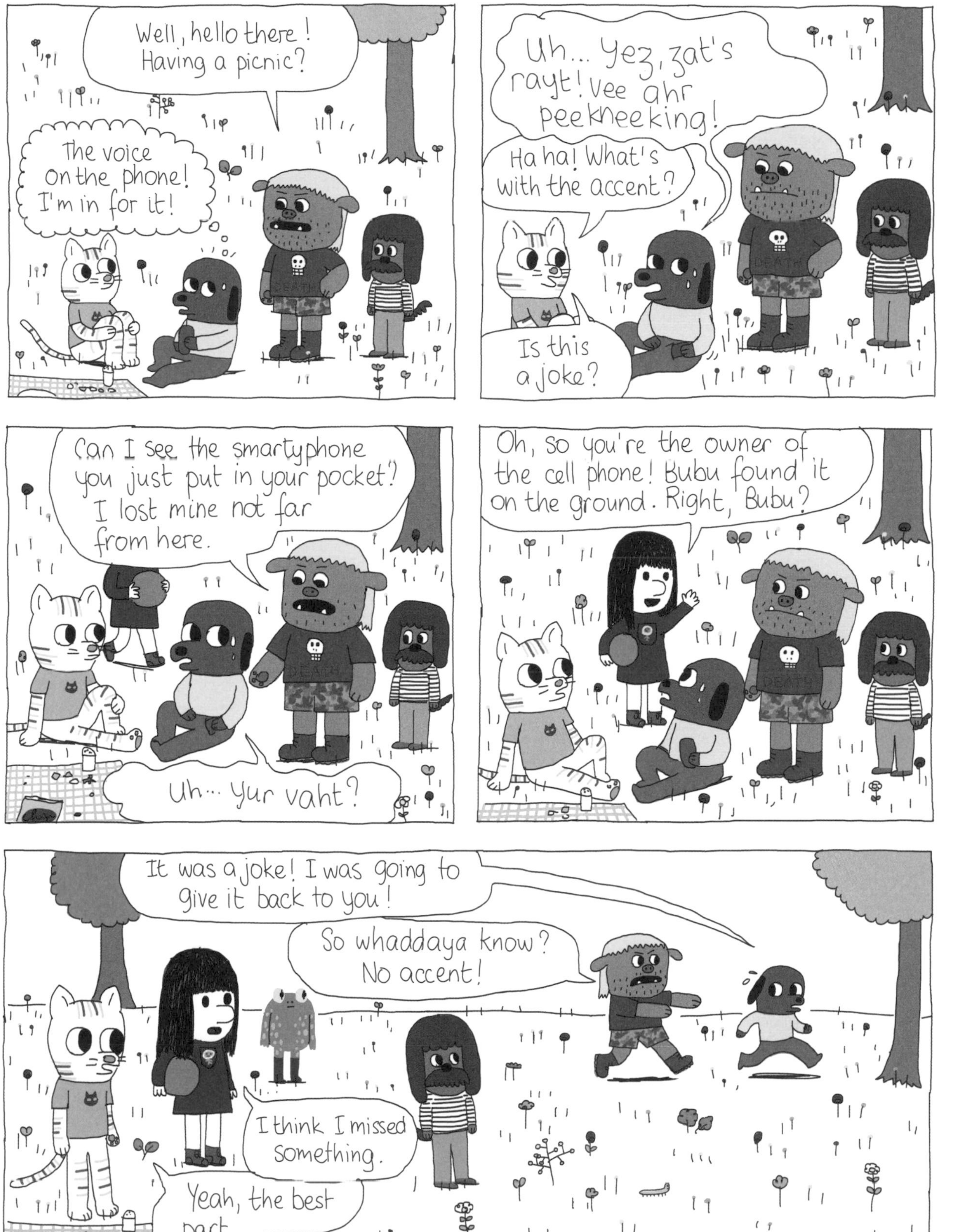
Well, hello there! Having a picnic?
The voice on the phone! I'm in for it!
Uh... yez, zat's rayt! Vee ahr peekneeking!
Ha ha! What's with the accent?
Is this a joke?
Can I see the smartyphone you just put in your pocket? I lost mine not far from here.
Uh... yur vaht?
Oh, so you're the owner of the cell phone! Bubu found it on the ground. Right, Bubu?
It was a joke! I was going to give it back to you!
So whaddaya know? No accent!
I think I missed something.
Yeah, the best part.

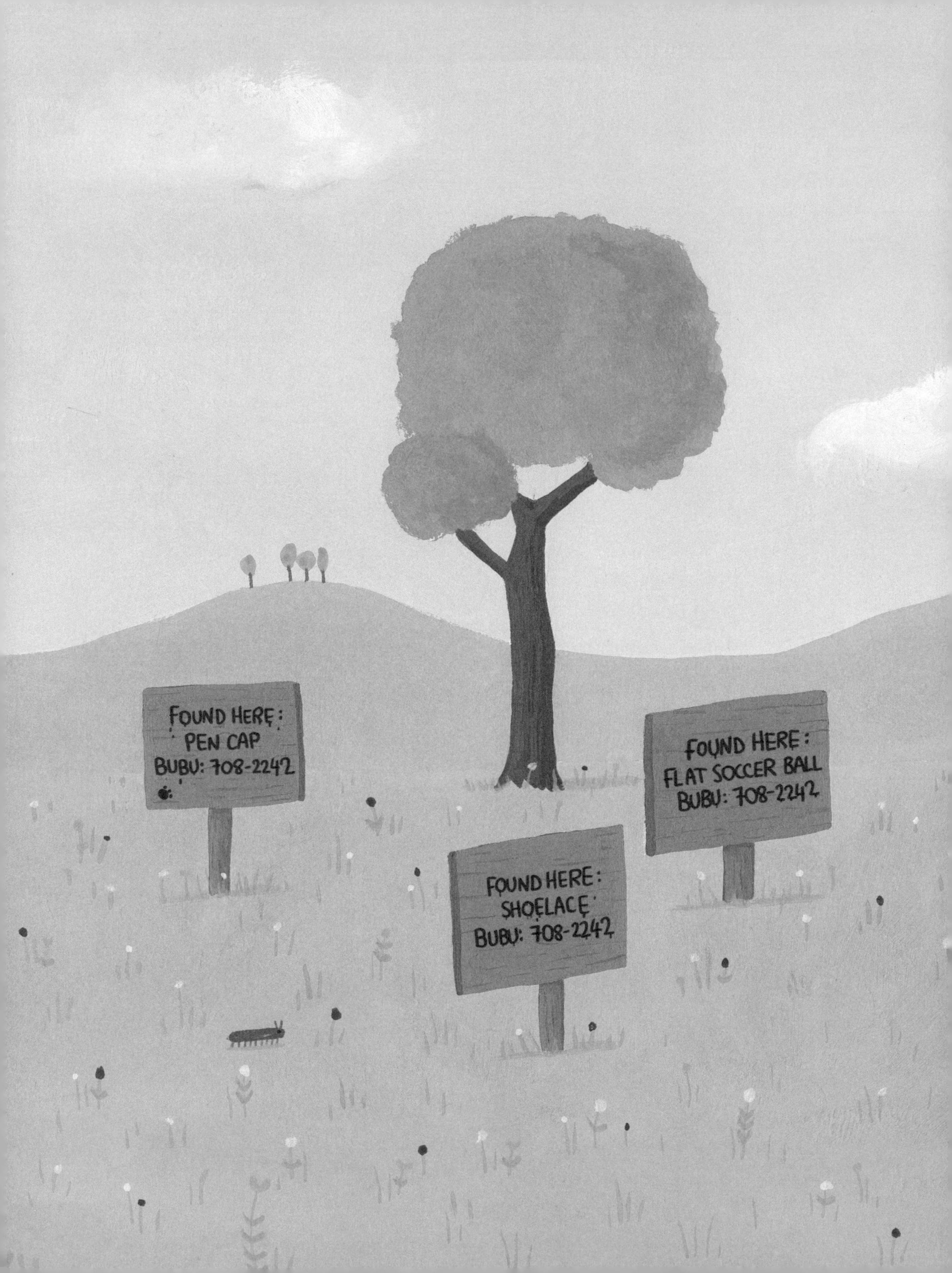
FOUND HERE:
PEN CAP
BUBU: 708-2242
FOUND HERE:
FLAT SOCCER BALL
BUBU: 708-2242
FOUND HERE:
SHOELACE
BUBU: 708-2242

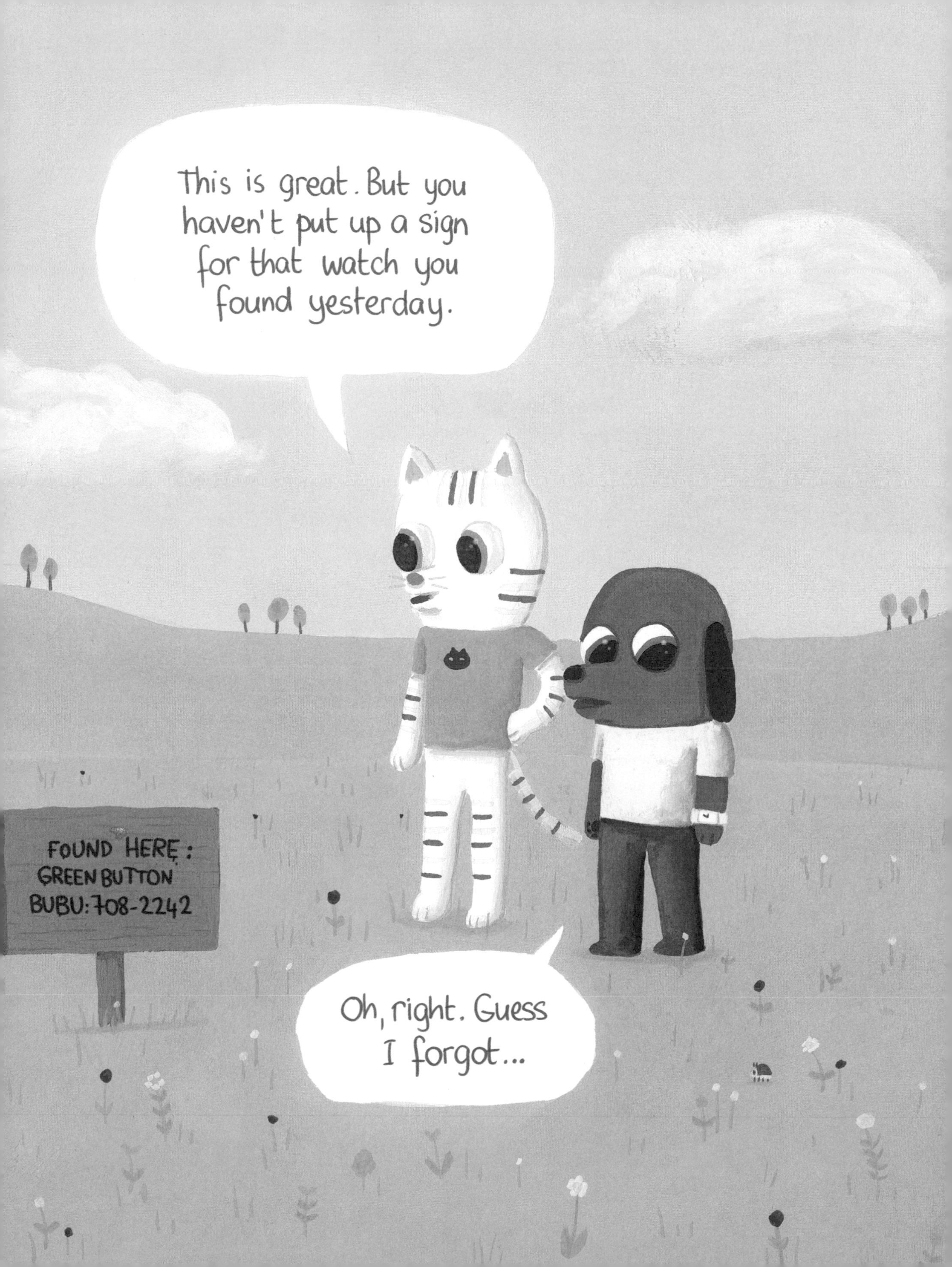
This is great. But you haven't put up a sign for that watch you found yesterday.
FOUND HERE:
GREEN BUTTON
BUBU: 708-2242
Oh, right. Guess I forgot...

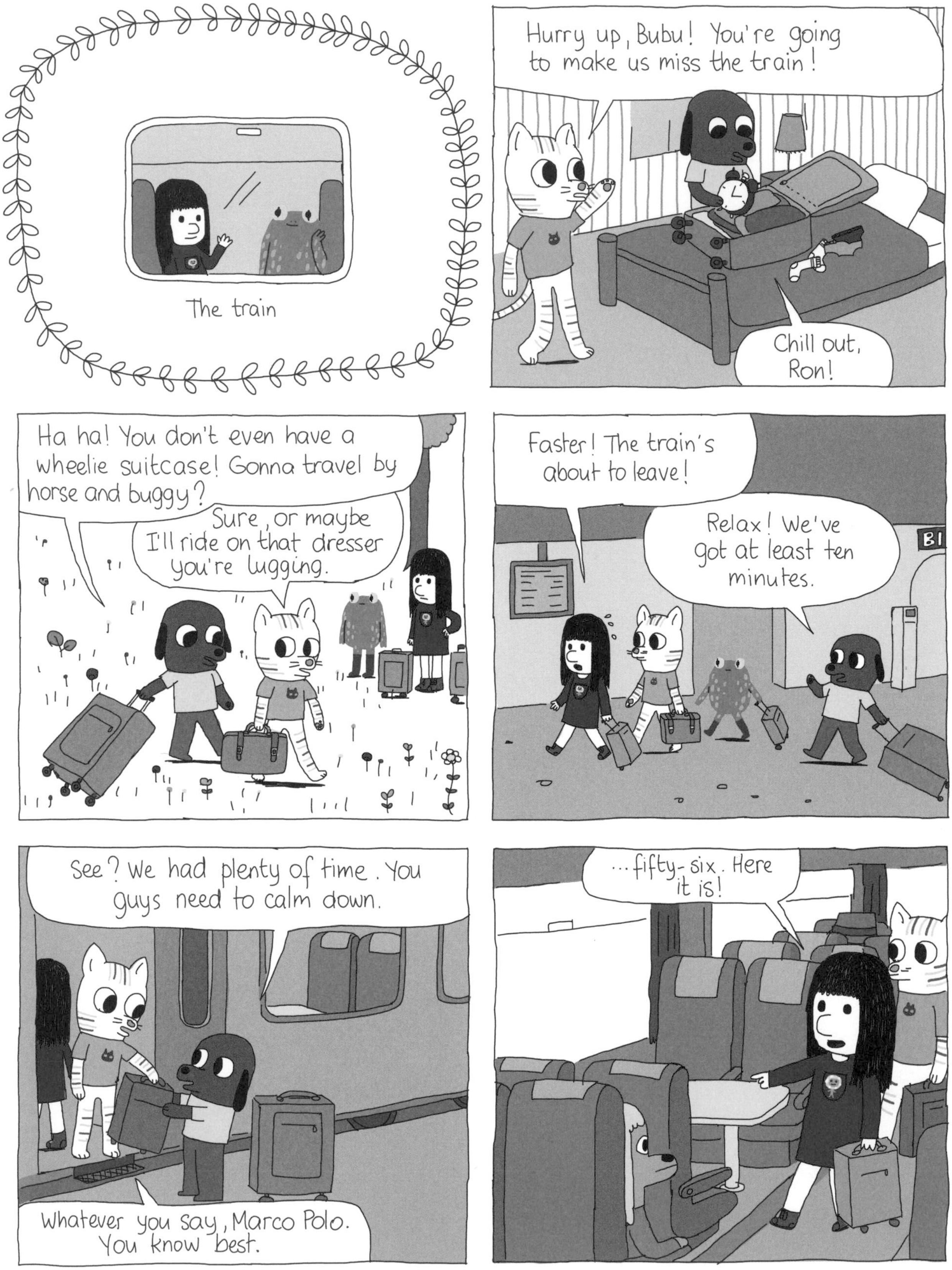
The train
Hurry up, Bubu! You're going to make us miss the train!
Chill out, Ron!
Ha ha! You don't even have a wheelie suitcase! Gonna travel by horse and buggy?
Sure, or maybe I'll ride on that dresser you're lugging.
Faster! The train's about to leave!
Relax! We've got at least ten minutes.
See? We had plenty of time. You guys need to calm down.
Whatever you say, Marco Polo. You know best.
...fifty-six. Here it is!

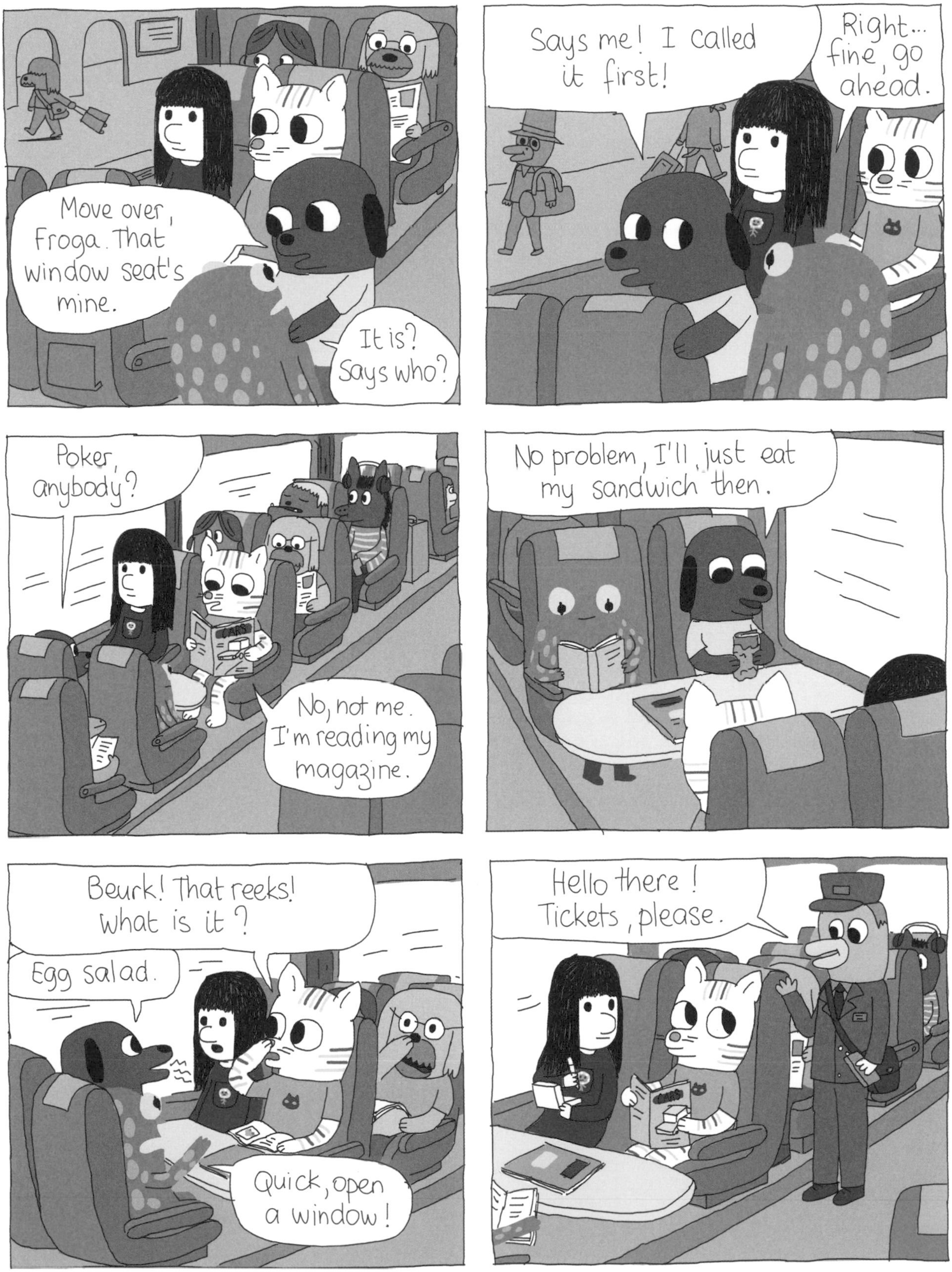
Move over, Froga. That window seat's mine.
It is? Says who?
Says me! I called it first!
Right... fine, go ahead.
Poker, anybody?
No, not me. I'm reading my magazine.
No problem, I'll just eat my sandwich then.
Beurk! That reeks! What is it?
Egg salad.
Quick, open a window!
Hello there! Tickets, please.

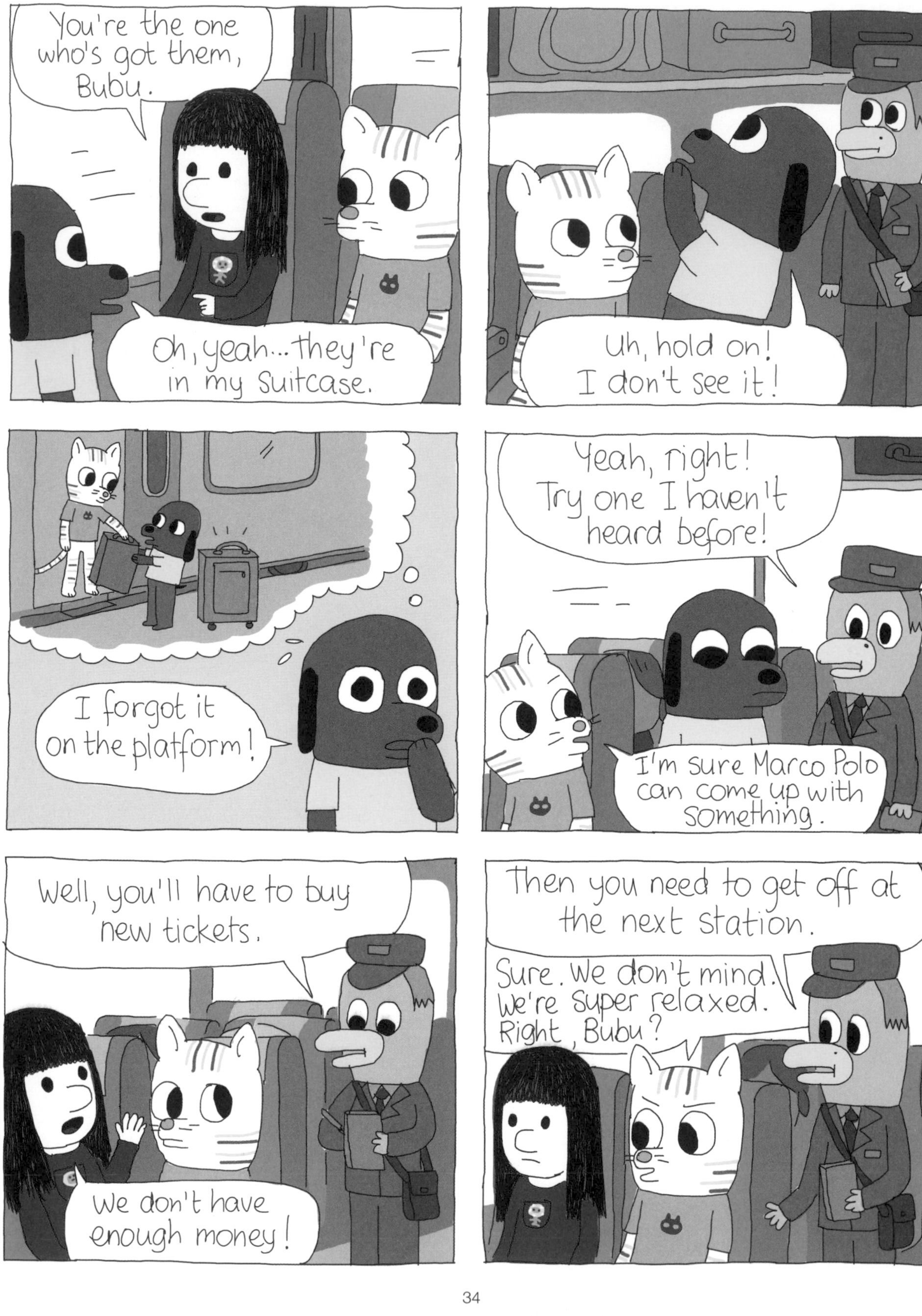
You're the one who's got them, Bubu.
Oh, yeah... they're in my suitcase.
Uh, hold on! I don't see it!
I forgot it on the platform!
Yeah, right! Try one I haven't heard before!
I'm sure Marco Polo can come up with something.
Well, you'll have to buy new tickets.
We don't have enough money!
Then you need to get off at the next station.
Sure. We don't mind. We're super relaxed. Right, Bubu?

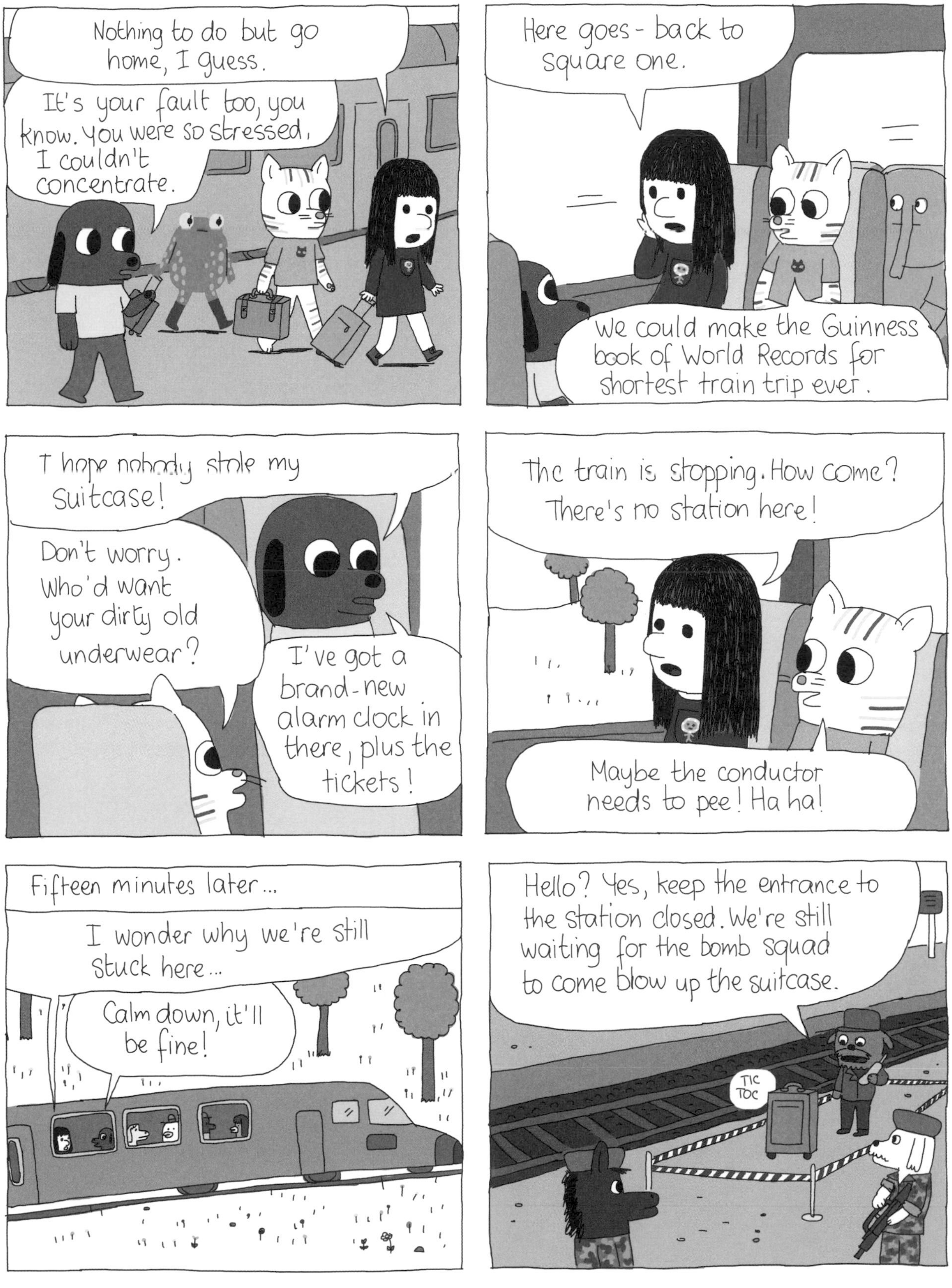
Nothing to do but go home, I guess.
It's your fault too, you know. You were so stressed, I couldn't concentrate.
Here goes - back to square one.
We could make the Guinness book of World Records for shortest train trip ever.
I hope nobody stole my suitcase!
Don't worry. Who'd want your dirty old underwear?
I've got a brand-new alarm clock in there, plus the tickets!
The train is stopping. How come? There's no station here!
Maybe the conductor needs to pee! Ha ha!
Fifteen minutes later...
I wonder why we're still stuck here...
Calm down, it'll be fine!
Hello? Yes, keep the entrance to the station closed. We're still waiting for the bomb squad to come blow up the suitcase.
TIC TOC

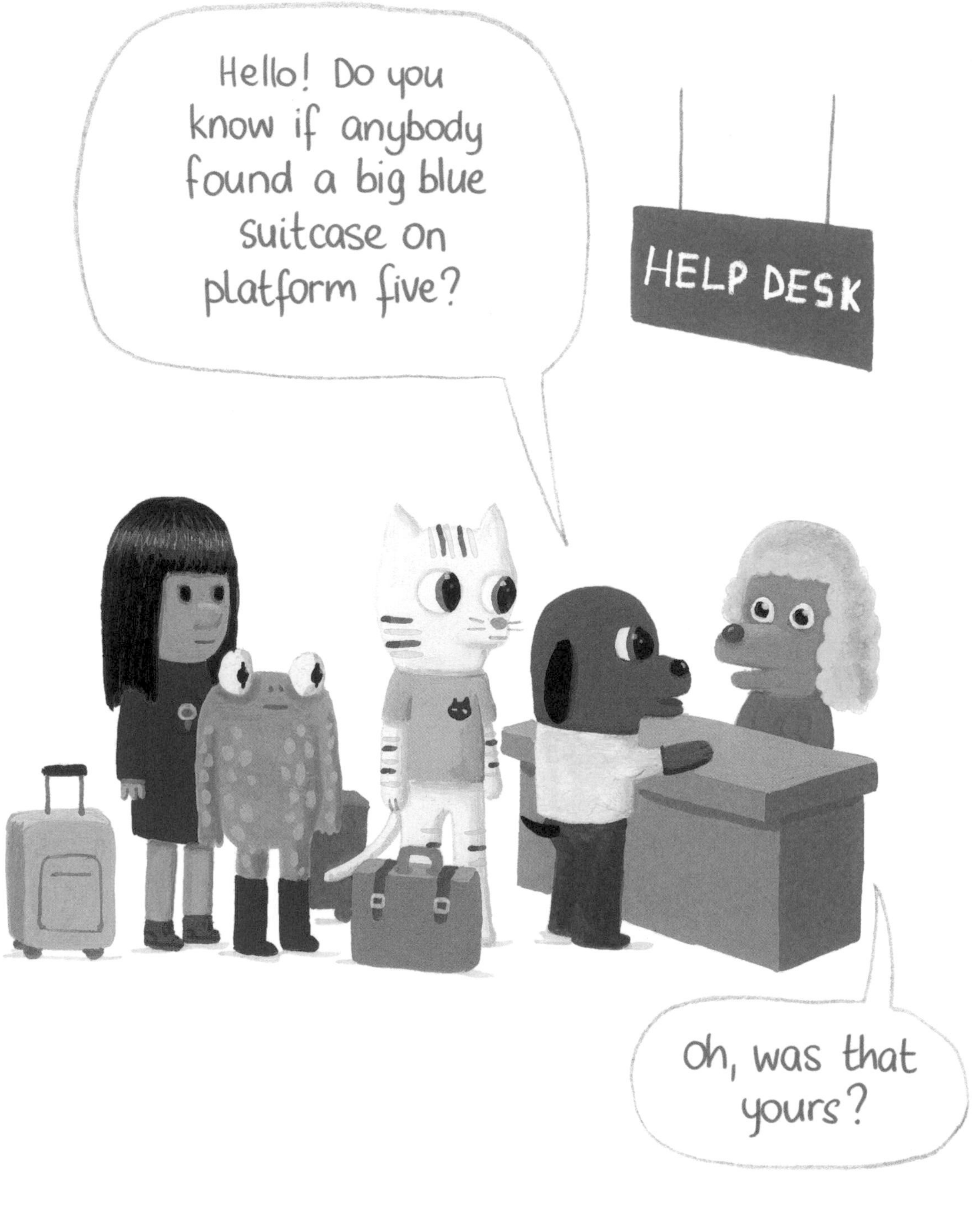
Hello! Do you know if anybody found a big blue suitcase on platform five?
HELP DESK
Oh, was that yours?

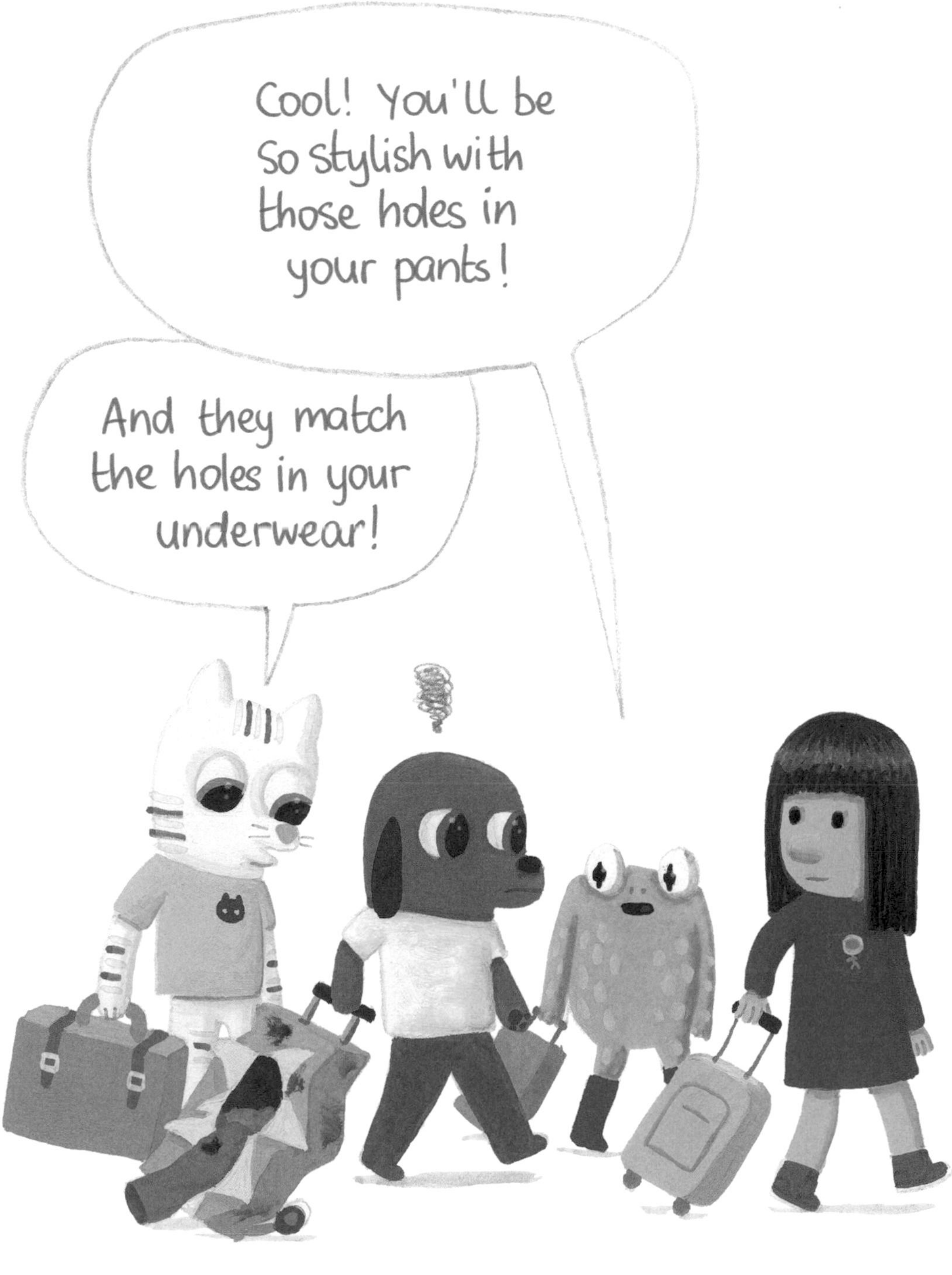
Cool! You'll be so stylish with those holes in your pants!
And they match the holes in your underwear!

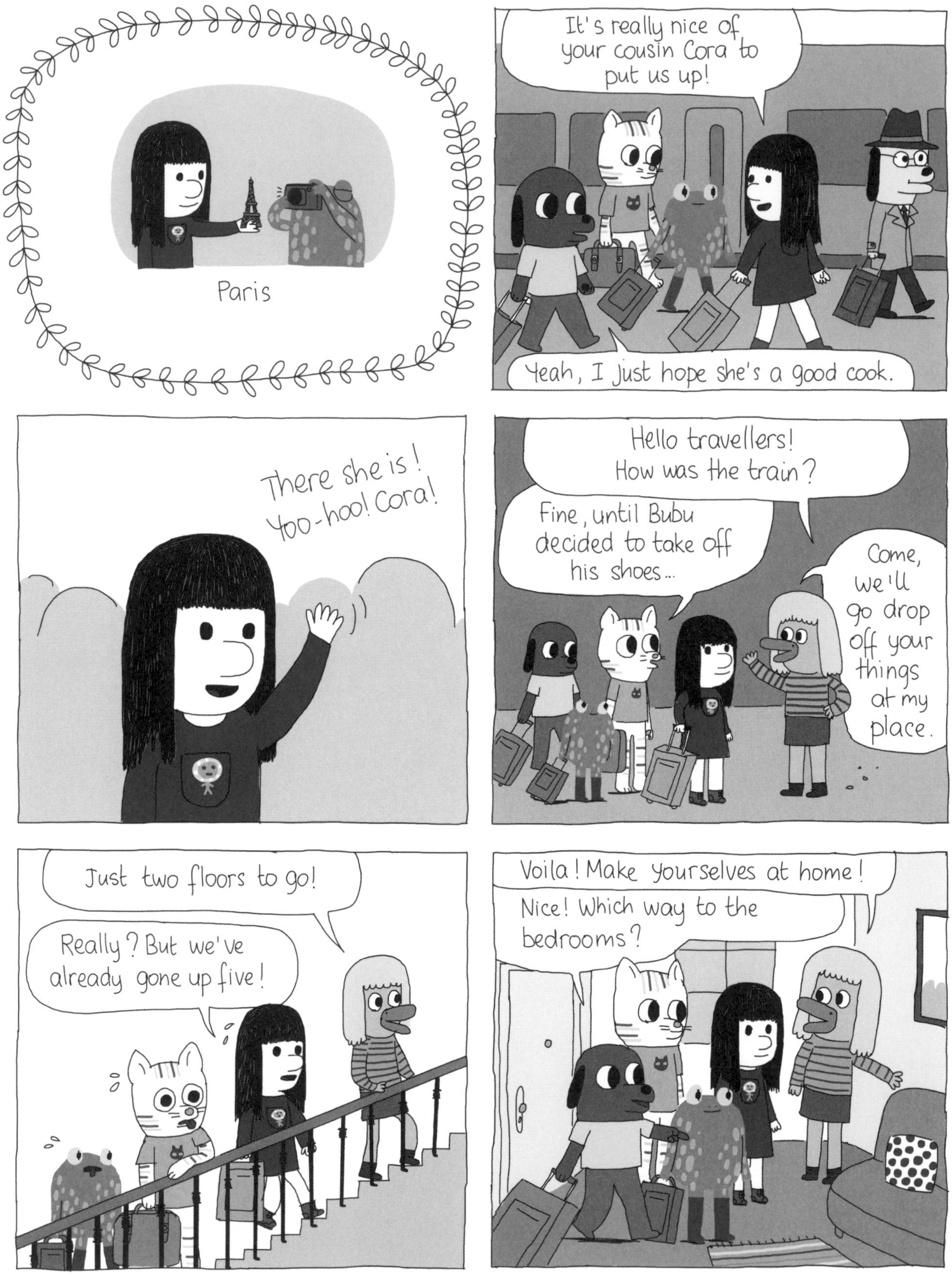
Paris
It's really nice of your cousin Cora to put us up!
Yeah, I just hope she's a good cook.
There she is! Yoo-hoo! Cora!
Hello travellers! How was the train?
Fine, until Bubu decided to take off his shoes...
Come, we'll go drop off your things at my place.
Just two floors to go!
Really? But we've already gone up five!
Voila! Make yourselves at home!
Nice! Which way to the bedrooms?

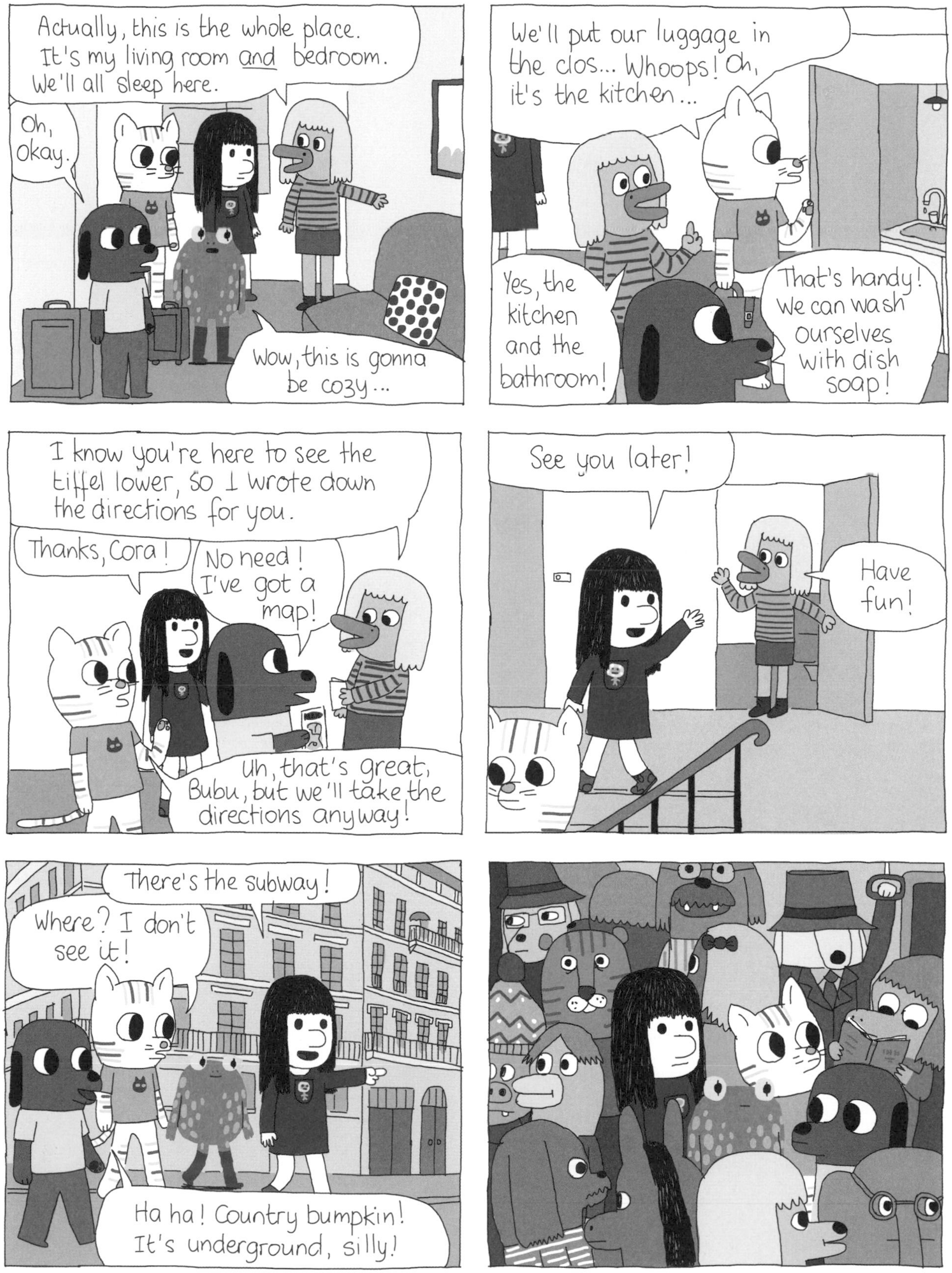
Actually, this is the whole place. It's my living room and bedroom. We'll all sleep here.
Oh, okay.
Wow, this is gonna be cozy...
We'll put our luggage in the clos... Whoops! Oh, it's the kitchen...
Yes, the kitchen and the bathroom!
That's handy! We can wash ourselves with dish soap!
I know you're here to see the Eiffel Tower, so I wrote down the directions for you.
Thanks, Cora!
No need! I've got a map!
Uh, that's great, Bubu, but we'll take the directions anyway!
See you later!
Have fun!
There's the subway!
Where? I don't see it!
Ha ha! Country bumpkin! It's underground, silly!

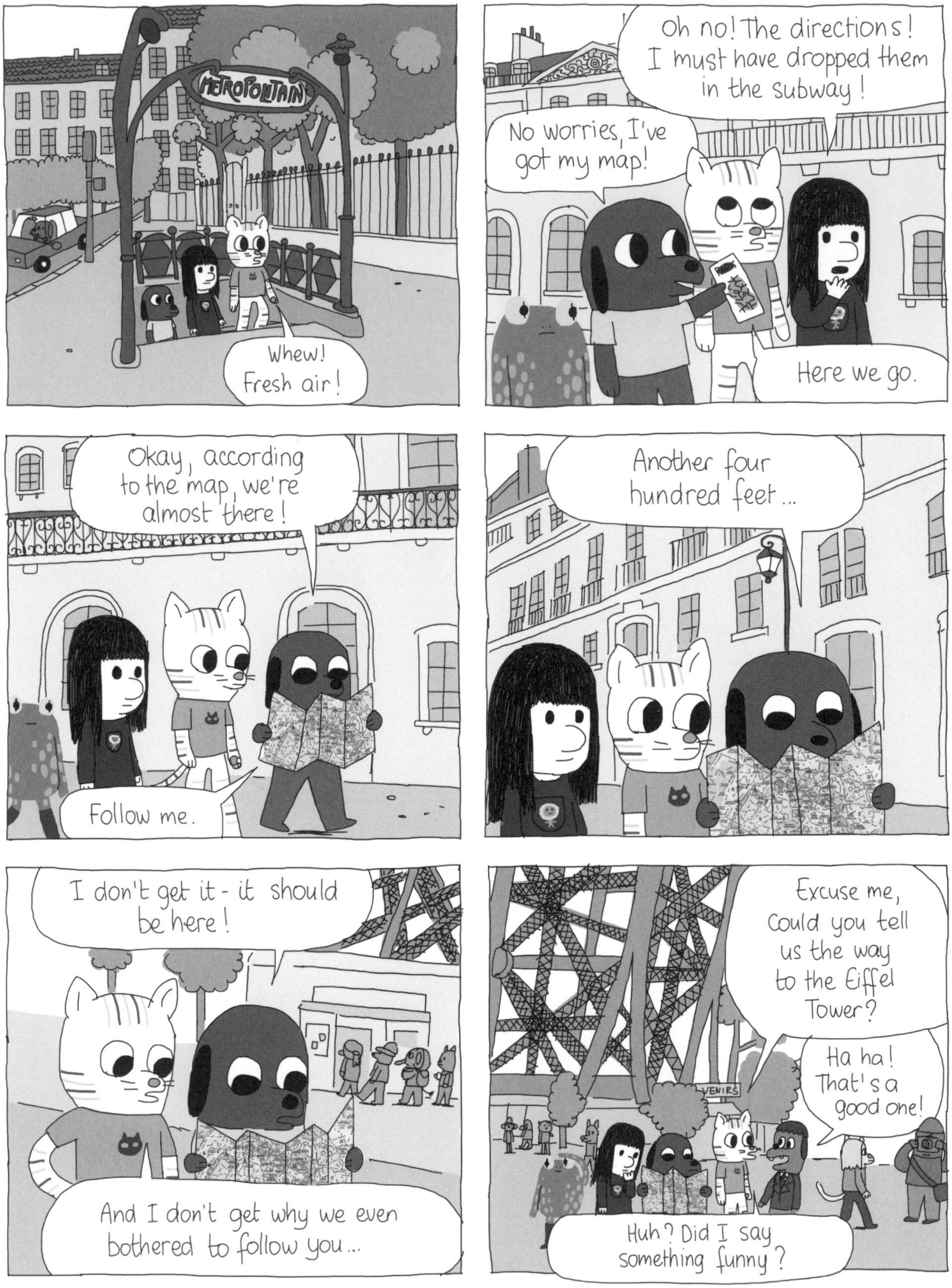
METROPOLITAIN
Whew! Fresh air!
Oh no! The directions! I must have dropped them in the subway!
No worries, I've got my map!
Here we go.
Okay, according to the map, we're almost there!
Follow me.
Another four hundred feet...
I don't get it - it should be here!
And I don't get why we even bothered to follow you...
Excuse me, Could you tell us the way to the Eiffel Tower?
Ha ha! That's a good one!
Huh? Did I say something funny?

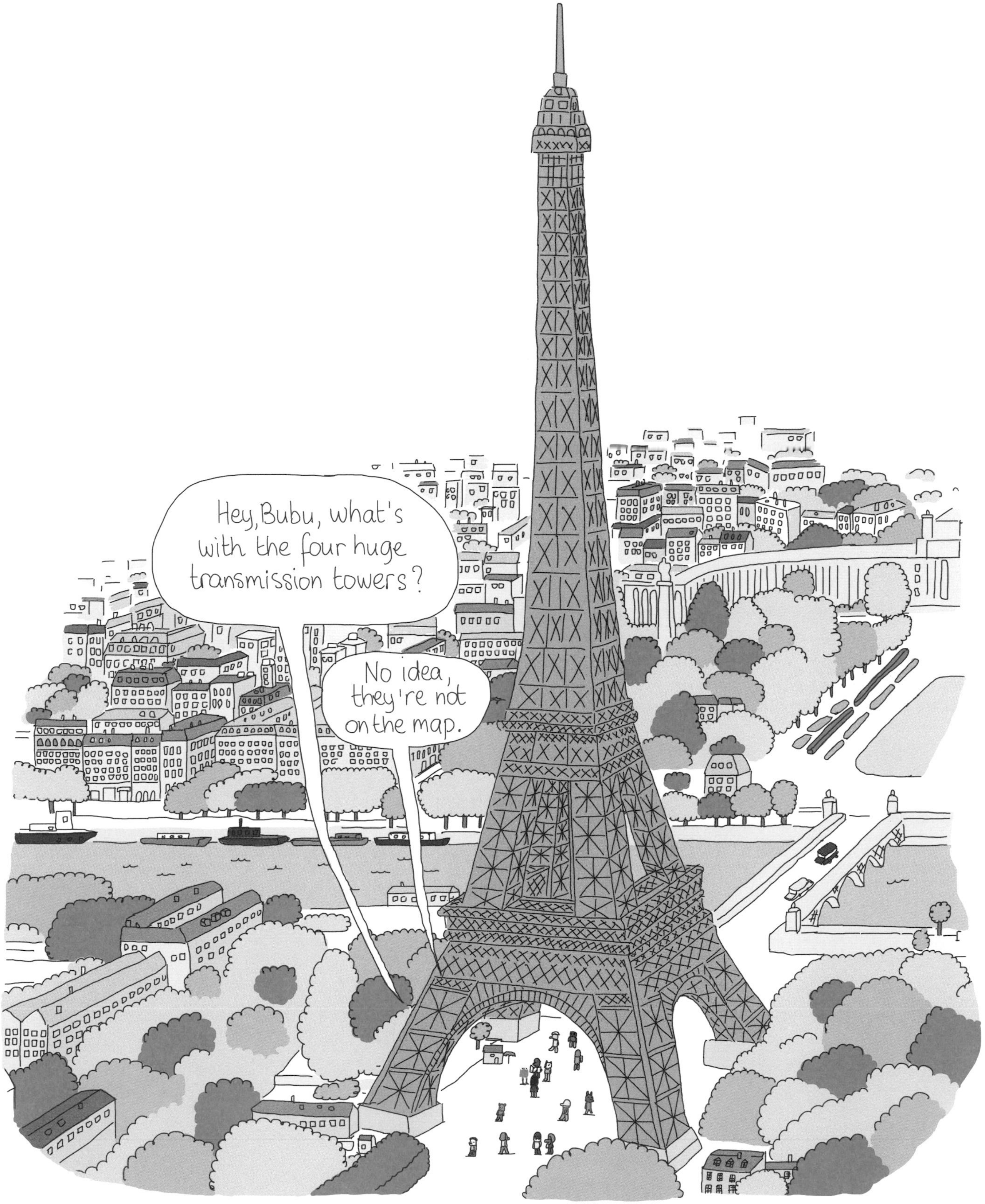
Hey, Bubu, what's with the four huge transmission towers?
No idea, they're not on the map.

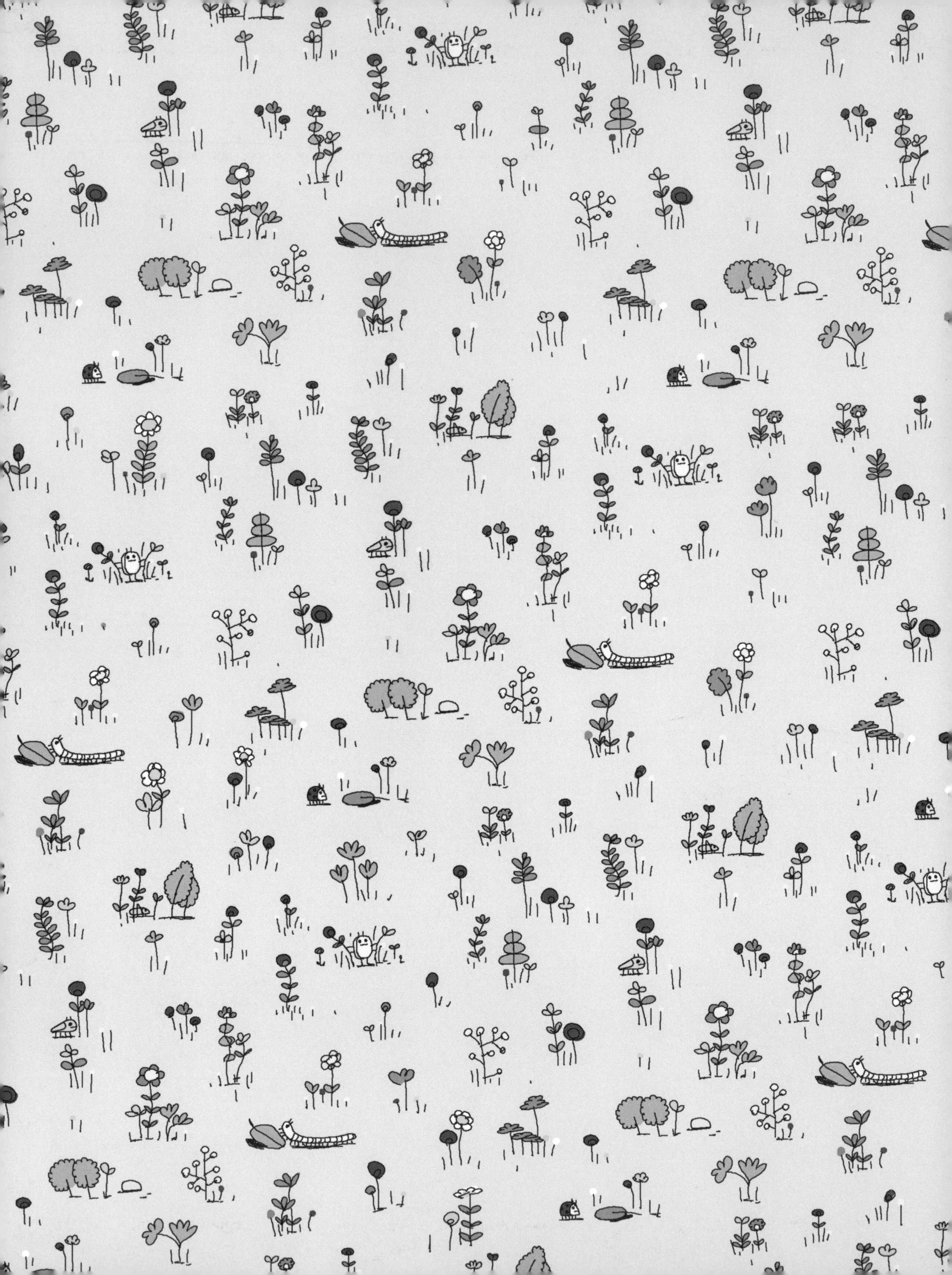